Katharine Sarah Macquoid

At the Red Glove

A novel. Part 3

Katharine Sarah Macquoid

At the Red Glove
A novel. Part 3

ISBN/EAN: 9783337051150

Printed in Europe, USA, Canada, Australia, Japan

Cover: Foto ©Andreas Hilbeck / pixelio.de

More available books at **www.hansebooks.com**

AT THE RED GLOVE.

A Novel.

BY

KATHARINE S. MACQUOID,

AUTHOR OF "PATTY," "LOUISA," ETC.

IN THREE VOLUMES.
VOL. III.

SECOND EDITION.

LONDON:

WARD AND DOWNEY,

12, YORK STREET, COVENT GARDEN, W.C.

1886.

PHŒBE.   " Good shepherd, tell this youth
          What 'tis to love.
SILVIUS.   It is to be all made of sighs and tears;
           It is to be all made of faith and service;
           It is to be all made of fantasy.
           All made of passion and all made of wishes;
           All adoration, duty and observance;
           All humbleness. all patience and impatience;
           All purity, all trial."

SHAKESPEARE.

CONTENTS OF VOL. III.

CHAPTER II.

CHAPTER III.

CHAPTER IV.

Part VIII.—The Fly Escapes.

CHAPTER I.

CHAPTER II.

CHAPTER III.

CHAPTER IV.

CHAPTER V.

Part VI.—On the Brink.

AT THE RED GLOVE.

CHAPTER I.

A HARD FIGHT.

"I have said too much unto a heart of stone,
  And laid mine honour too unchary out:
  There's something in me that reproves my fault;
  But such a headstrong potent fault it is,
  That it but mocks reproof."
                                        SHAKESPEARE.

THAT perception or power of appreciation set forth in the old saying, "Eyes and
no eyes," is surely not an altogether mental
quality; the feelings play their part in
it, and when these are adverse to enjoyment or weighted by some fear, they dull
all power of receptivity; they are as
unimpressionable as unprepared glasses;

B 2

should a photographer offer these to the sun to paint on, they remain blank; the sun may reflect pictures thereon, but these can make no abiding impression.

Marie felt the pleasant warmth of the sunshine this morning as she came along the streets to the " Red Glove " for breakfast, but she had no eyes for the light and shade on the houses and under the arcades, for the glow of the flowers in the balconies of the Hôtel Beauregard; she did not notice the sparkle on the fountains and on every salient object to which the glowing light was wishing a good morning.

Last night Madame Bobineau had parried the girl's questions; but Marie had insisted on an explanation of what had been said, and, carried away by the overwrought feeling produced by the scene in the glove shop, she had been vehement and very angry. She asked her cousin again and again what Captain Loigerot meant by trying to kiss her hand, but Madame Bobineau had only shrugged her shoulders and sneered at her vehemence. At last, ashamed and alarmed at the violence of her agitation, Marie burst into a fit of crying. She said she could not eat any supper, and the old woman rejoicing that so much food should be saved, wisely let her go home without remonstrance.

It seems as if all temperaments have their special uses. In the great drama called human life we have been inclined, perhaps formerly more than at present, to overestimate the worth of a warm heart as compared with a cold one; yet there are cases when a cold temperament is very useful to its possessor and to others. It may be said there are phases in the life of each individual when it is far pleasanter and less irritating to be treated coldly than sympathetically. If Marie had been tenderly questioned and petted when Captain Loigerot left the "Red Glove," she would have probably lost all self-control, and have revealed all that she most wished her cousin to remain ignorant of.

Madame Bobineau's phlegm and seeming indifference to her tears roused the girl's pride. She felt that she was lowering herself in her cousin's opinion by showing feelings which the old woman could not understand, and she was forced to believe in Madame Bobineau's ignorance of the captain's admiration. She tried to turn away from the sudden suspicion which Loigerot's words had aroused, though she could not shake off the sorrow which had struck her down. The calm, however, induced by the girl's belief in Madame Bobineau's ignorance and want of observation, did not last through breakfast.

Marie felt very stupid this morning, so much unusual emotion had caused reaction. When she reached the "Red Glove" its mistress was actually smiling; she kissed Marie, and remarked on the fineness of the morning; then she bustled forward into the kitchen, and gave the girl a triumphant glance as she saw her looking with surprise at the table.

Marie beheld a most unusual sight there. Over the edge of a white compotier hung purple and white grapes, and these supported a glowing crown of peaches and nectarines.

"See"—Madame Bobineau licked her thin lips—"how kind and thoughtful is Madame Carouge. In the midst of her own happiness she does not forget her friends."

Marie kept her face calm, but her heart ached dully, and it seemed to her that this was a pain that might go on for ever. She must hide her grief, too, from all, even from her sympathising friends at St. Esprit. She no longer wished to return there : how could she own to those pure, saintly women that she thought constantly of a man who did not love her?

"Ah ! even to tell them that would be boldness," poor Marie thought.

Her cheeks flamed as she went on thinking what would the sweet, kind Superior say of her "little girl," as she had always called Marie, if she learned that Monsieur Engemann had not even proposed friendship for her, while she actually desired the love of a man betrothed to another woman ; for he had not denied the captain's assertion about Madame Carouge, he had only, Marie thought, resented the familiarity of his congratulations.

" What makes you so rosy, child ? " said Madame Bobineau sharply. She had just consulted her watch, and she knew that before long the captain might be expected; she had a good deal of way to make with Marie before he came. The girl must be thoroughly prepared this morning; her reception of her future husband must not be left to chance. Yet the wary old woman scarcely knew how to begin on the subject. She knew so well that the upshot of persuasion often depends on its first sentence. She was looking keenly at Marie, when the girl raised her eyes, and a clue suddenly revealed itself to help Madame Bobineau.

"You should have worn your new gown." Then she went on, without waiting for an answer, "We shall not have a finer day than this, or a better opportunity for wearing it."

"I had not thought of it," the girl said drearily.

"It is not too late; finish your breakfast

quickly, you will have time to go back and change before we start, or we can call for you on our way. Monsieur le capitaine will like to see you well dressed."

Marie was silent, but her face became hotter.

"I do not wish to change my gown," she said. "I do not care for the captain's opinion."

Madame Bobineau stretched out her hand and helped herself to another peach, gobbling at it as if she meant to get advice out of its wrinkled brown stone; the juice streamed over her chin, and but for her table napkin would have reached the front of her gown; but while she pulled away the skin and deposited the red-veined stone on the edge of her plate, she gained a few moments for reflection. The time was so short that she felt the only way was to take Marie by storm.

"Do you know, you poor child"—there was a pitifulness in her voice that roused the girl's attention, it was so new—"I feel very sorry for you?"

Marie looked up quickly; she read intense scrutiny in the small, hard eyes fixed upon her face, but she would not wince. Unconsciously Madame Bobineau was developing this fresh, simple nature at high pressure. All at once it came to the girl, as by a sudden flash of knowledge, that it was safer to believe in the hard eyes, than in the pitying voice. She must take good care not to betray herself.

She actually smiled into the wrinkled face. "Don't be sorry, then, dear madame," she spoke gaily; "be glad that I am economical instead of vain, though, indeed, I hardly think that fat old captain's notice or approval would touch any one's vanity."

"Chut! chut! you are disrespectful;

Monsieur Loigerot is not old," said Madame Bobineau; "but I am not thinking of your gown in that way, Marie. I—I— well, child, I wish to spare your feelings if I can, but perhaps it is best to be candid; in your place I should do all I could to-day to seem gay and glad, and it may be if the neighbours see you going about smiling and well-dressed, they will forget what they know about you; it is not nice to be talked about and laughed at, my girl."

Marie was not red now; the colour that had come so quickly fled as fear took possession of her, and she felt suddenly cold and trembling.

"What does any one know about me? I do not understand you," she said, in a dull voice, while a hundred dreads seemed to be muttering words that her ears could not gather.

Madame Bobineau shrugged her shoulders.

" Ah, yes, what does any one know indeed? That is always what an imprudent girl asks. She is like the ostrich who I have heard tell thinks no one can see her if she hides her head in the sand. I will tell you what people know, Marie, it is what you have shown them so heedlessly. You forget, silly girl, that people have eyes as well as you, and while you use yours to show your feelings with, others look on and amuse themselves with the sight. I tried to check you at the bear-pit, but I hear you have since then been seen talking in the street with Monsieur Engemann when I knew nothing about it; you lay in wait for him, I suppose. Then, of course, last night we could see plainly what ailed you—at least, Monsieur Engemann and I could see. He might have been a little kinder to you, I will say, but you must make excuse for him; I dare say you do, now you have had time to think over his position and his hopes."

"Oh, madame!" Marie cried, putting up her hands as if to protect herself from the storm of words. But the old woman went on :

"What a lucky man he is, riches and beauty both waiting for him! If I had been you, I would have forced myself to congratulate him, instead of letting him see your own feelings."

The direct, merciless words robbed Marie of all perception. She felt stabbed, struck down ; she could only instinctively raise a shield against her adversary ; she must, she would, still hide her secret from her.

"What do you mean," she said slowly, "when you say I lay in wait for that gentleman? I met Monsieur Engemann by chance as I came here from my lodging, just as I have met Monsieur Loigerot several times, and Monsieur Riesen too."

She stared with angry defiance at the hard eyes that would not leave her face.

"Bah! bah!"—the old, wrinkled woman nodded and went on eating grapes—"you make a good fight, Marie, and I respect you for it. I like a girl to be brave and show a good face when she has made a fool of herself. Now be wise as well as brave, child. Do not let the gossips of the Spitalgasse say to-day: 'There's that poor little fool Marie Peyrolles going about with a sad face, and wearing the willow because Monsieur Engemann is away courting Madame Carouge.'"

Marie rose up, her eyes glowed with a strange light; no wonder it was strange: a new inmate had taken possession of the girl's heart; a feeling never yet evoked into life by the gentle, kindly nurture which had fostered all that was tender and sweet in her.

At that moment Marie hated Madame Carouge with the whole strength of her newly-kindled nature. The short, sharp revelation of last night had taken the sheath from her feelings, and left them ready to stab her to the quick, ready even, she thought, to work harm to others. She could have struck the cruel old woman who had thus stripped her bare to her own sight, and had shown her, as vividly as if she had held a mirror before her mental insight, the revelation of her feelings which her behaviour had made to Monsieur Engemann. She burned with shame and sorrow. This, then, was the explanation of his changed manner; he had seen her love, and pitying it, had striven to show her that it was unwelcome, and thrown away on him.

Marie had the romance of an unsophisticated nature, and it is possible that if this solution had not been offered by Madame Bobineau, she might have seen it herself, but under another aspect; she might have seen it as a proof of the nobility of Monsieur Engemann's disposition. He would not be false to Madame Carouge, nor would he insult her by a lenient pity for her feelings. He had pitied her; but he was straightforward in all things, and therefore he had not lost time in showing her the truth. But Marie was writhing under the consciousness that she had made herself ridiculous; she had been so overwrought last night that she had lost count of how she had looked and spoken, and fear as to how much she had revealed brought exaggeration with it to deepen her suffering. It was an exquisite agony to fear that she had betrayed her love; it made her feel that she could never again meet the eyes of Monsieur Engemann; and yet, as she stood thinking, a feeling which took the form of anger, but which was the voice of her outraged self-respect, recalled words and looks on his part which justified the attraction he had possessed for her.

"It is you who are not wise, madame. Yes, you look shocked at my plain-speaking; but you irritate me, and you must take the consequences. By what right do you say that I am going about with a sad face for Monsieur Engemann? I am young, and so is he, and young men and young women take pleasure in speaking to one another. Were you not young once yourself, madame? I do not care for the gossips of the Spital-gasse, or for Berne, they can say what they choose. I am not likely to stay among them. I shall go away as soon as I can hear of another employment," she said with flaming eyes.

Just now, drawn up to her full height, Marie looked as grand as the beautiful widow, and Madame Bobineau felt a little afraid of her; but the last words set her at ease again; they gave her a definite cause of quarrel.

"Bah! little fool"—she leaned back in her chair, and looked sneeringly at Marie from head to foot—"one would think you were on the stage, child, with all this fine talk. You will go away!—Bah! Have you forgotten that I am your guardian, and until you are of age you must do as I bid you? How can you go away? You have no money. And no one in Berne would employ you if I refuse to release you from your duties here? Even the Sisters dare not take you away from me if I assert my claim. But I fancy you do not feel in a mood for convent life just now, do you, Marie?" She looked so keenly at the girl that the rosy colour flew over Marie's face in a flash of bloom.

Marie's indignation seemed to make her taller, larger in every way, as she stretched out her strong, well-formed hand and arm toward Madame Bobineau.

"Are you trying to make me do something

desperate?" she said vehemently. "Oh, how wicked you are!"

Madame Bobineau smiled contemptuously.

"On the contrary, foolish child, I am very forbearing. I could have you put into the reformatory for such bad behaviour; and certainly, if you try to run away, I shall give instructions to the police to take you there, you ungrateful hussy."

The old woman's rage had flashed out at last, and it brought tears into her hard eyes.

The sight of the tears softened Marie. "I don't want to be ungrateful, but why do you say cruel, bad things of me?" Then, worn out, she flung herself sobbing into a chair, and covered her face with her hands.

Madame Bobineau let her cry in peace. At last she said:

"Come, be reasonable. I have not said bad things of you. On the whole I consider you a good girl, or I should not keep

you here, Marie. But I must judge from
what I see, and I consider you have been
imprudent and unguarded. Last night you
heard of Monsieur Engemann's engagement
to Madame Carouge, and, without considering what might be said or thought of you,
you burst out crying and sobbing like a
baby."

Marie remembered the vexation that had
caused her tears, and she knew that they
had not been only caused by the news she
had heard. She told herself bitterly that the
discovery of her own folly was too deep a
humbling to be got rid of in sudden tears.

"I cried because I was vexed with Captain
Loigerot. I—I don't like that old man, he
tries to kiss my hand."

Madame Bobineau felt that her time was
come.

"I tell you again that Captain Loigerot
is not old; and he is well-off and well-

mannered, and any girl in Berne would be glad to take him as a husband." She paused. Marie's hands had fallen in her lap; but now her mouth opened widely, showing her pretty, even teeth. "Yes, Marie, such a man as he is might marry any one he chooses; and he has chosen you, a poor, penniless girl; he is very fond of you, and kind to you, and instead of feeling flattered by it, you call him bad names."

Marie's stare relaxed; she leaned back in her chair and laughed out merrily.

"No—no, not bad names," she said; " but, madame, I only said he was old. What do you mean—Captain Loigerot has chosen me? Oh, the poor old dear! And is that why he gave me the bouquet? Why"— she jumped up again and stood erect—"it is absurd to talk of; he comes up to about here"—she touched her shoulder; "I can see quite over the top of his bald head; and

—and he is double my age. Oh! but it is too amusing."

She sank down in the chair again, and laughed till her eyes ran with tears.

Madame Bobineau was surprised at the girl's sudden change of humour, but she was far too experienced to imagine from this that she had conquered.

" He is an excellent match, and the good captain's kindness is unlimited," she said. " He found out you liked flowers, and he took the readiest way to show you he was devoted to pleasing you. He said to me : ' She shall have a flower-garden of her own, and a greenhouse also. She shall have good clothes and everything that I can give her, and she shall do nothing but enjoy herself, if I can only please her.' "

Marie jogged the foot she had crossed over its fellow, and made a wry face.

"And what did you answer the poor man?"

Madame Bobineau shook her head at the scornful tone.

"You need not mock, Marie. I told the captain you were difficult to please, and that I could not answer for your caprices; and I said he must be patient. All that was arranged before you accepted the nosegay."

Marie smiled.

"But listen, child. The captain asked leave to walk to church with us to-day, and after that he wishes to escort us to the Schänzli in the evening. Now, Marie, I myself heard you accept this last proposal."

"Well, and what if I did accept it?"

"I am going to tell you. You must look as nice as you can. People make themselves smart to go to the Schänzli. There will be music there to-night; you may as well get ready now. Do you not see that if you change your gown later on, the captain will have a right to think it is done for him?"

She looked anxiously in the girl's face, but Marie showed no signs of yielding.

" Go quickly, my child," the old woman urged, "and then if the captain comes before you return, I will take him to church, and you will join us there."

" Stop, madame " — Marie had been thinking. " I am not going to be led into anything against my will. If I go to church and come out with the captain, does it pledge me to anything ? "

Madame Bobineau was growing desperate ; her temper was rising fast. The captain would be here in ten minutes, and she had made no impression on Marie.

" You do nothing I ask you, and you are very deceitful. You have been trying to impose on me, Marie," she said angrily, "and you know it. What right had you to accept those flowers ? You knew fast enough what you were

doing—a beggar like you, indeed, to have
likes and dislikes! I have been much too
forbearing. Whoever heard of a girl choosing a husband for herself? I have chosen
you a husband, and all you have to do is to
accept him gratefully—voilà."

She took a large pinch of snuff, and mentally called herself an old fool for not having
taken this attitude earlier in the discussion.

Marie rose up.

"I do not want to be ungrateful or dis-
obedient," she said sadly. "I will go
and change my gown to please you; but
I cannot marry Captain Loigerot."

"Nonsense! You must marry him, I
tell you he is as rich as he is kind. What
more can you want in a husband?"

Marie turned away; her face was full
of sorrow. "I cannot love him, and how
can I marry a man I do not love?" she
said, half-crying.

At that moment, she really wished she could accept the captain ; it seemed such an easy escape from the glove shop, from her cousin, from Madame Carouge, and from her misery.

Madame Bobineau snapped her fingers.

"Love! bah! I said nothing about love. What can love have to do with your marriage ? A girl in your position. Marry for love, indeed ! that is a luxury that only rich people may indulge in. I don't believe there is such a thing except in foolish story books. A girl like you marries for a home, for a position, Marie, and Captain Loigerot can give you both. You little simpleton, do you think I married for love ? Do you think I took Bobineau for anything except his glove shop ?"

She had to soothe herself with an extra pinch of snuff.

Marie had reached the door of the

kitchen, and now she leaned her head against it ; she did not want the old woman to see her tears.

"My father and mother married because they loved one another ; I'm sure they did."

She murmured this as if to herself, but the old woman heard, and snorted with rage.

"And a nice pair of penniless fools they were all through their lives. And pray what happened ? They didn't take much by their *love*, Marie. They offended all their friends " —she rapped her large-boned knuckles on the snuff-box to keep time to her words — " and they died, as they had lived, beggars—yes, beggars, and left you to be brought up on charity. Don't talk to me of your father and mother, Marie ; their love was mere self-indulgence, it was a crime ; and you have no reason to be grateful to them for bringing you into the world, and leaving you without means of support. I should like to know what would become of you if I died to-morrow. I've nothing to leave, after my funeral is paid for, I can tell you ; you would have to starve, you ungrateful jade."

Marie raised her tear-stained face. Once more she stretched out her hand, but this time the gesture was an imploring one.

" Leave me alone, madame ; please let me be till after mass ; I cannot think all in a hurry while you are scolding me. I do not say that I will marry Captain Loigerot ; but I will think about what you have said."

She went out, her head bent on her breast. All life and hope had fled from her movements as she walked slowly back to her bedroom in the court at the foot of the steps.

CHAPTER II.

" Every temper, except downright insipid, is to be animated and softened by the influence of beauty."— *Tatler.*

"Les choses les plus souhaitées n'arrivent point ; ou si elles arrivent, ce n'est ni dans le temps ni dans les circonstances où elles auraient fait un extrême plaisir."—LA BRUYERE.

MADAME CAROUGE had sat silently gazing at the scene before them.

· The open summer-house, with pointed red roof, in which she had invited Rudolf to rest, was built on the top of one of two towers, at the angles of the old city wall, which reaches up the hill and supports and girdles in the terrace beside the flowery churchyard. The angle piers and roof of the summer-house were now rosy with clinging garlands of Virginia creeper. Just below was the old town-wall, so flower-and-weed-grown that its gray stones only peeped out here and there among the snapdragons and tufts of gray-flowered grass and ox-eye daisies ; houses clustered at the foot of the wall, and beyond them was the exquisite blue-green of the river ; on the left, high above, rose the huge dark pine-covered ridge that shelters Thun from the north wind ; on the right the willow-trees down by the river were silvery gray as they bent over an island clasped by the arms of the Aar—a curtain of trees, chiefly poplars, almost crossed the water—and beyond was the still, broad lake washing the feet of the Niesen and of the grand semicircle of mountains that seemed the advanced guards of the snowy giants above them.

The sky was still clear on this side, and the dazzling white of the Blumlis Alp and the Freundhorn made a vivid contrast to the rich green and purple of the Niesen and the flank of another ridge that stretched out as if to meet it; while filling up the gap with her silver glory was the Blumlis Alp—a glory now at midday tempered by delicate gray shadows; beyond, the Jungfrau, the Monch, and the Eiger rose up stupendous, as if in a kind of scorn of their lesser brethren. A wreath of vapour circled the Niesen; but it looked feathery, and as if the next gust of wind might blow it away.

Rudolf found it hard to believe he was gazing at sinful, sorrow-stained earth; he felt that this scene might be a glimpse into heaven.

" Surely," he said in a low voice, " there cannot be bad people in Thun, the sight of all this beauty must keep them pure and true, I fancy."

He did not look round. If he had seen his companion's face he would have realised the fact, so hard to grasp and yet a fact after all, that no one sees the beautiful in nature exactly as his fellow sees it.

While this exquisite scene had taken such complete possession of the man that he almost seemed winged, transported out of all grosser affections in the contemplation of its beauty, the woman had also looked at it with pleasure, but the effect on her had been different. The joy its beauty gave her had quickened her pulses, but it only made her long yet more impatiently for the earthly happiness which she felt was nearly hers. The change in Rudolf's manner made her almost sure that he would to-day ask her to be his wife. Madame Carouge loved too truly not to be timid about the love that might be offered her in return ; but although doubt was wounding, she told herself not to fear ;

the man who loved beauty as ardently as
Rudolf Engemann appeared to love it,
could not fail to love her when she was
once his wife. And so her eyes had soon
left the lofty, dazzling Blumlis Alp and
its neighbours and had settled on the face
beside her—far more beautiful to her in
that moment of exquisite enjoyment than
anything in heaven or earth could be.

Before either of them had spoken,
Riesen's harsh voice broke into the stillness. "My good friends, let us go, we
ought to move on, we are late as it is;
the boat people will think we are not
coming."

Engemann and Madame Carouge started
at the interruption; this movement annoyed
the clock-maker and amused his wife.

"Is it not lovely?" she said; "I see you
can hardly tear yourselves away. Ah! that
is so natural—what it is to be young!"

She gave a deep sigh, then, turning to her husband, she said briskly, " We must go down the broad steps, Lorenz; that is the shortest way, you know."

They soon reached the principal flight of steps leading down into the town, and while Madame Riesen stopped behind to raise her skirt, her husband went on and placed himself once more next Madame Carouge. It seemed to him that in asking Engemann to seat himself beside her, and then remaining so long alone with this young fellow in the summer-house, the widow had completely thrown aside restraint, and had treated her other companions with scant courtesy.

Now they recrossed the bridge, and, turning to the left, they followed the Aar, past the garden of the quaint old Freienhof, past a house or two nestled among close-growing trees, then beneath a winding

avenue which cast exquisite green shadows
here and there, barred with golden sunshine ; the river that bordered one side
of the sequestered path was deepest blue-
green, into which some willow-trees reflected
themselves grayly.

Now an island parted the river into two
embracing arms, and on it was a boat-house
wreathed in vines, and these, golden as the
sun touched their leaves, painted themselves
in yellow on the still water.

Now the path diverged a little; they
passed a vine-covered châlet so bowered in
climbing plants, that one wondered how
the outside wooden shutters could ever be
closed. Through the vine-leaves that gar-
landed the windows, orange nasturtiums
and red geraniums were glowing, and over
the shed on one side a Virginia creeper had
already turned to vivid flame-colour.

Gardens with fruit-laden trees lay between the path and the river; and then all at once they came to an open space, a grassed church-yard with crosses wreathed with flowers, and mounds covered with loving tokens. In the midst of all a little church reared its slender red-capped tower, the white walls so richly clad with roses and flame-coloured leaves that under the glowing light they seemed to burn.

A narrow path led down to the river outside the low boundary wall of the church-yard, and this was so covered with leaves that the stones were invisible. Here was a little landing-place between the church-yard on the left, and on the right a lovely garden gay with flowers.

A gaily-painted boat, with red cushions and a striped orange-and-red awning, was waiting here for its expected freight.

A strip of grass parted the church-yard from the river, and this was bordered by clumps of brilliant flowers interspersed with stately hollyhocks, the blossoms on their tall spires, crimson, yellow, and creamy white.

Engemann had walked along in too absorbed a state to notice Madame Riesen's chatter. There had been something dream-like in the subdued light in the avenue, in the unreal tints on the water, and then in the sudden vision of the slender church tower rising out of its nest of circling trees, and its hedge of flowers beside the water.

But when they drew near the landing-place, Madame Carouge stood still till Rudolf came up to her. She pointed to the many-coloured screen of hollyhocks and tall marigolds through which showed the river and the town, surmounted by its castle and church, and framed by the dark pine woods stretching on till they seemed to reach the lake.

"Yes, it is all most beautiful," said Engemann, and then he offered his arm to help Madame Carouge into the boat.

But here he was superseded. A strong brown hand grasped the arm of Madame Carouge, and a broad, upturned red face showed merry blue eyes and a row of strong white teeth.

"You are welcome, lady," the sturdy boatwoman said. "I began to think you were not coming. Attention, Aline!" she said to the oarswoman.

By this time, Monsieur and Madame Riesen, Engemann, and the widow were all seated. Just as Madame Carouge saw that she should be compelled to take a seat beside the clock-maker, she also saw a means of escape.

"Change with me, Monsieur Engemann," she said. "You and Monsieur Riesen are the heaviest, and I shall feel safer if you sit together in the middle."

And Rudolf seated himself between Riesen and Madame Carouge. The clock-maker scowled; in his heart he called the widow some very ugly names.

The girl Aline, a young, good-looking likeness of her mother, but equally brown and sturdy, seated herself between a pair of heavy oars. She was bare-headed, but her face was tied up in white linen.

"Only the toothache," the mother said, in answer to Madame Riesen's question. "She is not yet accustomed to the damp from the river."

The mother, herself, standing erect in the stern of the boat, shaded by a round, black hat, looked completely weather-proof as she drove her long pole into the wall of the garden terrace, and pushed the boat out into the stream.

Soon they had floated past the little wall covered with flowers that reached the water's edge, and all at once the lake opened before them, broad and still, with mountains rising out of it as far as eye could reach. The higher line of snowy Alps had veiled itself now with clouds, and the purple pyramid-like Niesen was only partly visible, the wreath of vapour that had circled it reached to its top.

"Niesen has got his night-cap on," the clock-maker said, "but the day may be fine in spite of that."

The boatwoman did not answer; she was looking at the handsome couple, and she decided in her own mind that they were made for one another.

She had been sharp-witted enough to understand Madame Carouge's manœuvre in changing her seat, she enjoyed the clock-maker's discomfiture, and she began to talk volubly to him so as to distract his attention from the pair of lovers as she considered

them ; and her questioning compelled him
to talk in return.

So they glided on ; the awning sheltered
them. from the glare, but the heat was
oppressive ; the air seemed to be holding its
breath, listening for some sound to break its
stillness.

Madame Carouge raised her eyes, full of
soft languor, to her companion's face.

"Is not this happiness exquisite ?" she
said, in a low voice.

"Yes, madame, it is perfect."

But Engemann did not want to talk, and
he went on dreaming. He could not have
said what his thoughts were, for there was
little sequence in them ; perhaps at that
moment he realised the enjoyment of a lotus-
eater. It seemed to him delightful to drift
silently on and on amid this ever-changing
beauty ; the only jar in it being caused by
the voices of the clock-maker and his wife.

When sometimes he looked at his companion, he felt that she perfectly harmonised with her surroundings; her eyes, her attitude, were full of languorous repose.

But this appearance of repose was deceptive; there was fire under it. Already she was chafing at Engemann's continued silence, she could not understand his cold reserve, and her feelings rose in protest against it, but she resolved to leave him to himself.

"If he cares for me," she thought, "he must speak."

Engemann was quite unconscious of her impatience, he did not dream of the passion he had kindled; after his troubled night and his sorrowful waking, this afternoon had brought sweetness and peace; he felt steeped to the lips in blissful rest.

So they glided on.

CHAPTER III.

TEMPTATION.

"Accuse me thus; that I have scouted all,
Wherein I should your great deserts repay;
Forgot upon your dearest love to call,
Whereto all bands do tie me day by day."
SHAKESPEARE.

As the boat crossed the lake, Time proved the truth of Rosalind's adage; it travelled at divers paces with the several persons beneath the awning.

Rudolf Engemann was utterly unconscious of Time's progress; Madame Carouge was fevered with impatience that so much was being wasted, Madame Riesen wished to prolong it so that Lorenz might recover his temper; while to the clock-maker the hours had seemed leaden-footed ever since he and his companion had taken their places in the train, and he gave a grunt of satisfaction when they came in sight of Oberhofen, with its tiny bay, ended by the projecting point, its church, and ancient castle, with the range of mountains for a background.

Madame Carouge roused a little when she saw this charming picture; to her the time had gone by too quickly. Riesen had ceased to answer the boatwoman, and there had been a long silence. Meantime the widow had dreamed away her opportunities, and had lost her chance of speaking to Monsieur Engemann.

"I am a simpleton," she thought; "what is the use of all the trouble I have taken if I make no use of this chance? And yet——"

She looked at Engemann, and her courage would not come to help her; what

could she do ? She had given him his chance
and he would not take it, she felt shy of
him, fearful of losing his good opinion if
she did more. Was he one of those men,
she wondered—she had heard of them—
who lose all the prizes of life because they
are too unready to snatch at Opportunity
as she passes before them ?

" How cold and quiet he is ! " she said
to herself. " Is it that he enjoys this
beautiful scenery so intensely, or is it—— ? "

She frowned and turned to look into
the water, for she had met Madame
Riesen's eyes fixed on hers. The frown
drew those thick eyebrows together with
a threatening aspect which alarmed the
clock-maker's wife, and forced her to take
refuge in full cackle with the boatwoman.

Madame Carouge saw her own beautiful
face reflected in the water, and her brows
relaxed, her red lips curved into a smile.

" My love makes me distrustful," she

thought. "Marie will certainly marry the captain, and then——" She sighed, but she did not turn to look at Rudolf. She told herself that nowadays no man married for love; why did she expect him to be different from others? "And I have so much besides myself to give," she said bitterly. "But he need not be so cold, so reserved. Ah! it is, doubtless, my fault; I am so selfish, I so fear to betray my own feelings, that I have repelled him."

She turned toward him.

"Monsieur Engemann," she said softly.

Engemann started from his reverie.

"Yes, madame," he answered, smiling.

She gave him back a smile, but there was sadness in her eyes. "Pardon me, I disturbed you. You were thinking of something—something very interesting?"

She looked again into the water, and spoke in a low voice.

"I beg your pardon "—he turned to her

so that their faces were hidden from their companions — "I was thinking that we never get what we wish. It seems as if there were always a check on the will; even this water leaps up against the shore, and then it is called back." He sighed; his eyes were still fixed on the water: he was uttering his thoughts aloud.

To Madame Carouge it seemed that these words had suddenly swept away the barrier that had held them apart; her eyes grew darker and more liquid, and her rich complexion glowed more deeply as she earnestly looked at him.

She answered, in a low and tremulous voice : "But is not this check, as you call it, sometimes self-imposed? Do we not deceive ourselves? You are wiser than I am, monsieur; but I fancy self-distrust has before now come between a man and that which might make his happiness."

The tender, pathetic tone touched him, but it roused him too. He felt that something lay hidden in her words.

" What does she mean ? " he wondered, and he felt bewildered. " Does she mean that I have neglected my chance of pleasing her ? . . . How handsome she looks ! . . . Why do not I talk to her ? I am not doing my duty." . . . " On the contrary, madame," he said, " it is you who are wise and kind also; and this is a delightful day you are giving us; I am so greatly enjoying it, that I fear I have been selfishly silent; but I always am silent on the water."

Madame Carouge turned away abruptly. " Just the same as ever," she thought; " he always slips out of any personal talk, and drifts into commonplace : how cold he is ! " Then aloud : " Monsieur Riesen, shall we go back now or on as far as Gunten ?"

The clock-maker looked toward the farther side of the lake, and shook his head sagaciously. A bank of clouds showed black behind the Stockhorn and its range of followers, and the upper part of the Niesen was invisible.

"What do you think of the weather?" the clock-maker said to the boatwoman.

At this she looked sideways, and she also shook her head. "There is no telling, monsieur; it may come soon, or it may not come before night, but there is rain up there."

"It will be better to return, will it not, madame?" Riesen pointed to the heavy clouds.

"I suppose so, if you think there is rain coming?" She spoke sullenly.

It seemed as if the clouds had settled on her also. And, indeed, she felt that the happiness she had so burningly looked

for had been mirage. She had been all
day with Rudolf Engemann, and yet they
would probably part at the end of it only
as good friends as usual, they would not
have come any nearer to one another.

" You have enjoyed the day, I hope ? "
Rudolf said.

She looked bright and happy as she
answered, " I ?—I have found it only too
short."

" I think so too," he said, and then she
saw him smile as he looked across the boat.

Madame Riesen was struggling into an
enormous cloak, and, as her husband had
begun to put it on her the wrong side
out, a fretful dispute had arisen which
completely occupied the pair.

The widow turned again to Rudolf.
" A holiday seldom comes into my life," she
said, " and I have feared that a holiday
with a sympathetic friend must be one of

E 2

the things I should never know ; but to-day
I have learned that almost perfect happiness is possible."

A puzzled look came into the young
fellow's' eyes—novels had not been in his
way, and he wondered at her earnest
manner ; but the pathos of the last words
reached his heart.

"Surely," he said, "your life has not
been, is not always unhappy."

Madame Carouge's eyes filled with tears.
"Ah," she sighed, "I thought I had at
last found a friend who had learned to
read my feelings, but sorrow makes one
exacting. Do you not think it is more
dreary, more unhappy to live *alone* among
others than to live actually in solitude ?"

Engemann was much moved and puzzled
by her words and manner. He saw that
somehow or other he had grieved this
deeply-interesting woman.

"Perhaps," he answered, and then he sat in perplexed silence while the boat was rapidly rowed toward Thun. He felt that Madame Riesen was looking at him, now that she was cloaked and at rest, and under her inquisitive eyes he could not carry on the conversation which had aroused his curiosity as well as his sympathy.

The clouds had rapidly covered the sky, and presently heavy, scattered drops began to fall on the awning of the boat; the smoothness of the water was ruffled, and the golden glow left it as the sunshine was hidden by the fast-moving clouds.

"We had better go right on as quickly as possible to the landing-place near the Freienhof," Riesen said to the boatwoman, "the storm will burst almost directly."

"May I not wrap you in this?" Rudolf said to the widow, taking up a cloak. He

spoke so gently, with so much tender sympathy, that once more joy and hope came
back to her.

But now the rain beat down so heavily
that talk was impossible, and by the time
they reached the landing-place the opposite
side of the river was only visible through
the sheets of rain which poured down into
the troubled, turbid water.

"Take my arm," Rudolf said, and then
he hurried Madame Carouge along the
narrow covered bridge over the weir and
through the little garden to the coffee-room
of the hotel—the shortest way to the upper
floor of the quaint old house.

The rain was pouring down in a torrent
into the open court-yard of the hotel, and
the leaves of the plants climbing up the
pillars of the surrounding galleries were
already soaked with water.

The landlord's daughter, a kind-looking

graceful girl, and a tall, handsome maid in Swiss costume begged the two ladies to come into the kitchen and take off their wraps before the glowing fire there. Madame Carouge had escaped the rain better than her companion had, and she soon found her way to the salle, leaving Madame Riesen in full talk with the landlord's daughter.

Rudolf Engemann was in the salle alone, looking out of one of the broad, low windows. The dark hill opposite, across the river, was almost hidden by long cloud-wreaths moving so rapidly from one point to another that it seemed as if some battle were being fought up there. But the young fellow hardly noticed the strange effect outside, he was suffering a kind of remorse for the indifference he had shown in return for the widow's kindness. He looked round when the door opened, and, turning

away from the window, he came quickly
up to Madame Carouge.

"I am afraid we shall not get our walk
in the pine-wood," he said.

"Should you have liked it? I thought,"
she said, timidly, "you had, perhaps, found
the day long enough. I feared I had bored
you with my confidences."

Engemann reddened.

"On the contrary, I have been greatly in-
terested; but——" he hesitated, and looked
simply into the beautiful eyes fixed on
him—"I am not ready-witted, or much
used to talking in company, I cannot easily
put my thoughts into words; but what you
have said about the sadness of your life
troubles me deeply."

"Then I wish I had not spoken of it;
you must forget it, my kind friend, or I
shall feel that I was selfish."

Rudolf shook his head, and as she seated

herself in one of the window recesses, he placed himself beside her.

"This sorrow has come upon you since your husband died?" he said tenderly. "You were very young to have such a grief laid on you."

She drew herself a little away, and the soft glow vanished from her eyes.

"No, monsieur: I must tell you the truth, even if I lose your precious sympathy. I —I never loved my husband—I married for a home—not for love—it is true I was a mere girl—my husband was quite middle-aged—I—well, I tried to do my duty; but when he died I could not sorrow, I could only feel that I was free."

Engemann hardly knew what to say in answer, but her eyes asked him to speak.

"In that case," he said, "I wonder that you, so young and beautiful as you are, should not have married again."

Madame Carouge sat very erect and looked at him with a slight smile.

"I will tell you, my friend—for I may call you so now—why I have remained a widow. When I married, I knew nothing of love; I was an ignorant child; my husband gave me luxuries which were all new to me; but I soon tired of them, as children tire of toys, you know. One day he brought me home some romances, and I read them; then, monsieur, I learned how two souls in perfect unison can make for each other a heaven on earth; then I learned that I had myself destroyed my chance of happiness."

Her voice had sunk lower and lower; her eyes were fixed on her hands, clasped in her lap. She was looking sadly at her wedding-ring.

Rudolf, deeply stirred, bent over her, eager to hear the end of this, the first romance that had been confided to him by a woman; and, as he gazed into her beautiful face, his pulses quickened.

"Surely," he said, "a heart like yours can never be in need of love; there must have been many before now who have striven to win you."

"Yes, it is true," she gave him a sudden glance; "but I resolved to wait till I met one who loved me for myself. One knows when one is truly loved."

"You must know," he said earnestly.

She raised her eyes suddenly, and met his glance full of warm light; her own fell at once.

"I know nothing," she murmured. "What can a woman know? She only feels—and—loves."

The last word was scarcely audible, and yet Rudolf heard it; but he also heard the door open, and he saw a group of people come in, not only the clock-maker and his wife, but half-a-dozen English tourists on their way to Interlaken, grumbling about the rain-storm which had stopped their journey.

Part VII.—At Odds.

CHAPTER I.

A RESOLUTION.

"In delay there lies no plenty;
    Then come kiss me, sweet and twenty."
                                SHAKESPEARE.

THE church was so full when Marie reached it that she could not find a place in the nave, so she turned aside and knelt down before the altar of one of the side chapels. The poor girl was so absorbed in sorrow that she gave little attention to the service; she covered her face with her hands, and soon tears streamed between her fingers. After a while she looked up and saw dimly that the chapel in which she knelt was dedicated to " Our Lady of Sorrows." She took comfort at this; it seemed as if she had been led directly to sympathy; but she drew a long quivering breath as she accepted the omen. The deep stillness that stole over her spirits made the voices at the high altar sound far off and indistinct; but this stillness was not mute to Marie; it told her to submit, it warned her that a young girl could not venture on a life of struggle, and issue from it unscathed; it told her, too, that she would serve God better and more easily in peace than in strife; but still the means of obtaining this peace in her outward life was as distasteful to her as ever. . . . Once more she hid her face between her hands and bent her head in prayer.

"I am stubborn and rebellious," she sobbed, as she knelt on in troubled silence.

All at once she began to wonder what the Superior of St. Esprit would have counselled. Well, supposing she were once more at the convent, what had she to ask? Whether she should obey Madame Bobineau? And then Marie remembered the way in which the kind Mother used to question her on her mental troubles till they set themselves straight; she knew that in this case the question would have been asked, "Has Madame Bobineau a claim on your obedience?" And mechanically she found herself answering, "Yes, she is my employer and also my near relative."

Marie knew that the Superior would tell her disobedience was a sin, and at the thought her motive for this disobedience obtruded itself. "I disobey because I covet the love of a man who has none for me, who loves some one else." The words seemed to be whispered by a serpent. This was worse than the quietude of her sorrow, for the serpent-whisper stung sharply and the pain felt like poison, but she knelt on . . . still in mental struggle.

An old man, standing not far off, wondered at the absorbed piety of the young girl who never once stood or sat as others did, but knelt on like some old devotee. He noted, too, that though she seemed to be praying, she did not say her rosary or open the book she had placed on the ground beside her. : . .

The sermon was over; the most solemn part of the service began, but Marie took no heed. . . . All at once the bell rang, and she started. It rang again, three times, and every one in the church knelt reverently.

Marie bent lower still and tried to worship. Now at last she was able to fling away every thought of self and to remember where she was. . . .

The mass was ended. Marie rose from her knees and looked round. People were already moving, and near her—so near in the crowd that filled this southern aisle that Marie wondered she had not seen her before—was Madame Bobineau; and close by the old woman, in the act of rising from a chair, was Captain Loigerot. He did not see Marie, but the girl was impressed by the look of goodness on his face—it was full of happy peace. She gave a little gasp; was this an answer to her prayer? If she consented to marry this kind, amiable man, should she indeed go back to the happy, calm life she had so little prized at St. Esprit, but which she had learned to regret so lovingly? But then a flood of unwelcome thoughts rushed in. Marie's lips quivered and her eyes filled with tears. . . . " But if it brings peace," she murmured ; and she turned to follow the crowd out of the church.

Sharp-eyed Madame Bobineau had seen Marie, and she waited near the door till the girl approached. As Marie dipped her fingers in the holy-water stoup the captain stepped forward and did likewise, giving her a silent, smiling glance, as he touched her finger-points with his own stumpy digits.

" H'm ! "

A sudden clearing of the throat made Marie look up and become aware that Madame Webern, the confectioner, was surveying her with significant eyes.

Presently they all stood together on the pavement outside, while the scorching sun poured down a fierce greeting on the uncovered head of the captain as he bowed low to Marie before offering her his arm.

She looked at him a moment; she
shivered, and a cold, dull feeling took
possession of her; then she put her fingers
within the close clasp of his coat-sleeve;
Madame Bobineau took his other arm, and
they started. By that mute action the girl
told herself that she had made her sur-
render; that she had consented to accept
this man for her husband, a thought,
Divine in its unselfish truth, had urged
on her decision. Her prayers had cleared
away the mist of anger which Madame
Bobineau had awakened. Marie felt sure
that Monsieur Engemann wished her well,
and it seemed to her that if he had discovered her feelings towards him it must
make him happier to see her married to
a good man than left to drudge on at
the "Red Glove," pining for the love he
could not give her.

The mental struggle she had gone

through had exhausted her, and she did not know what the captain had talked about till they were near home. Then she began to listen.

"Tut, tut! Do you see it, mademoiselle? The day is clouding over; it will be vexing if our evening at the Schänzli is not bright. There will be music and many people; and you would like to see the Alp-Gluhen, would you not? I am sure you would like it, and the sky must be bright for that. Ah!" Here the captain managed to rub his hands together. "That is, let me tell you, mademoiselle, a sight which will rejoice your heart, seen from the Schänzli."

"Yes," Marie said, and she smiled.

After all, what did it matter where she went? She could never be happy again; but she could be brave, and she could try to make others happy; she thought this in the exaltation to which she had brought herself. She preferred, however, not to meet the captain's admiring eyes more often than she could help, and the street was so full of people coming and going that she had plenty of excuse for looking about her.

At last they stopped at the door of the "Red Glove;" the two elders stood still, and they let Marie pass in before them.

"I feel like a bird going in at the door of its cage," the girl thought.

But she went on to the kitchen and took off her hat; then she put the backs of her cold hands against her cheeks and felt how burning hot they were; she could not see the exquisite rose-colour that glowed on her face; her eyelids, it is true, were heavy, and her eyes were languid, but Marie had rarely looked so attractive.

Meantime Captain Loigerot was speaking to his landlady. He had had time to reflect upon his position, and although he still felt rather shy of the young girl he hoped to marry, a certain instinct warned him that it was better to adopt a masterful manner with Madame Bobineau.

"I may consider the affair arranged, madame," he said, "and I may now salute mademoiselle as my fiancée."

His little eyes twinkled greedily.

"I am sure I don't know about that," the old woman answered. "Marie is very young, and full of convent prejudices. She——"

The captain snapped his fingers.

"Ta, ta, madame, we will endeavour to overcome the convent; in your presence, however, be it understood."

He stood aside ceremoniously to allow her to pass him in the narrow passage, and Madame Bobineau went into her little sitting-room. She looked round, and then, not choosing to expose herself to another dispute with Marie, she went to the door, when she had offered Captain Loigerot a chair.

" Marie, Marie," she called out. She was saying to herself: " Will he expect breakfast? It is certain that he has not yet taken breakfast."

Her face lengthened, and sadness spread over her as she pictured to herself the treasured sweetbread and the half chicken, now lying snugly in her cupboard, being swallowed by the captain with the appreciation of a man who eats well every day; they would be completely thrown away on him.

" Surely Marie is as one of the plagues of Egypt to me," she said to herself. " It will indeed be a deliverance when the captain takes her to himself. Marie!" she called again, and she tried to make her voice pleasant, " Marie, come here, child, you are wanted."

But Marie did not come, and Madame Bobineau felt that she must fill up the gap of silence, lest the captain should take offence.

"Monsieur has breakfasted ? " she asked.

" No, madame, not yet "—he waved his hand pompously—" on so important an occasion as this, one must even derange one's habits. Mademoiselle Marie is worth such a sacrifice."

He looked up at the ceiling and cleared his throat. Though he was in love, he felt hungry, and he wished Marie would soon appear.

Madame Bobineau's face became browner and more puckered than usual.

" Will monsieur permit me to offer him a humble meal ? I——" every word seemed to drag itself out of her with pain.

Captain Loigerot waved his hand in refusal, but he bowed in acknowledgment.

"A thousand thanks, madame, but my breakfast is waiting for me at the hotel," he said, in his bluffest voice.

The captain rubbed his hands in self-congratulation. He had never eaten within the walls of the "Red Glove;" but it seemed to him that in accepting Madame Bobineau's hospitality even in Marie's company, he should make a disastrous exchange for his comfortable and ample repast at the Hôtel Beauregard.

Marie came in shyly, and stood still in the doorway.

The captain got up. He had set down his hat beforehand, and now he gravely walked up to the girl, and, partly standing on tiptoe, he said, "Permit me," and he kissed first one rosy cheek and then the other with infinite satisfaction.

"Mademoiselle Marie," he said, "I will do my best to make you happy."

Madame Bobineau stood open-mouthed with wonder and curiosity at what would happen—but wonder conquered.

For Marie did not resist the captain's salute, or run away afterwards; she was quite passive. She blushed still more deeply, and then all her newly-gained colour left her, and she looked very white as she sat down on a chair near the door.

The captain had turned rather red at his own daring, but now he rubbed his hands cheerfully.

"Monsieur must be very hungry," Bobineau said; she was human, after all, and she pitied Marie at that moment.

"It is true, madame, I am hungry; but I had forgotten it." He turned from his contemplation of Marie, and plunged his hands first into the bottom of one pocket,

then of another. "And—and—I have also
forgotten—Diable!" he muttered, "it was
not a thing to forget. Mademoiselle Marie,"
he bowed stiffly, "I wished to offer you a
token of—of friendship, but I have unfortu-
nately left it upstairs. If you will permit
me, I will go in search of it."

Marie looked at him fixedly. "Certainly,
monsieur, as you please."

Her tone was as lifeless as her attitude,
but the captain admired what seemed to him
her self-possession. He had had some mis-
givings about the giddiness natural to
girls, but Marie appeared to him to have
accepted her new position with the dignity
which would have been natural to Madame
Carouge.

As he left the room to go upstairs, Madame
Bobineau bustled out after him, and Marie
was left alone.

While she had stood in the kitchen

nervously twisting her fingers together,
she had felt as if that which she knew lay
before her were impossible to undergo ; and
then, by a sudden wrench, she had forced
herself away from the kitchen-door against
which she had leaned, a tall, trembling
figure, clad in her pale gray gown, and
had come, as it were, recklessly into the
captain's presence.

How simple an act this so dreaded
kissing had been ! And yet . . .

For an instant her blushes had seemed
to burn into her cheeks, and then she had
grown cold as a stone. It had been a mere
formal action, and yet Marie felt as if she
could never again be the same ; she was
irrevocably parted from Monsieur Engemann ; even if he were free she had put
a barrier between them ; through those
kisses she belonged to Captain Loigerot.

And now she sat still in a kind of

stupefied despair, while Madame Bobineau
hurried out and followed the captain
upstairs.

"Excuse me for intruding, monsieur,
but have the goodness to listen to me for
a moment," she said, as she stood at the
open door of his sitting-room.

He did not ask her to enter. A sort of
impatient surprise met her in his small
eyes; he considered that she was imper-
tinent to have followed him.

"At your service, madame; but it is a
pity you should take the trouble to climb
the stairs when I intend to rejoin you below
directly. I—" and he took a small parcel
from his table, and puffed out his words
with extra effort—"I only came to seek a
gift I wish to offer to Mademoiselle Marie."

He waited for Madame Bobineau to
precede him down the stairs; but she did
not move, she stood still fully relieved

against the white painted door, looking even
more like a brown toad than ever. "Pardon,
madame," he said, and he stepped past her.
He was going downstairs, when he felt
pull at his coat-tails.

He turned round quickly.

"Madame——" he began.

"Chut!" She put her finger to her lips.
"Will it not be wise if monsieur has his
breakfast before he sees the child again?
Marie is a little confused, it is all so new
to her. We will dine in monsieur's absence,
and Marie and I shall attend vespers, and
then we hope that monsieur will honour us
with a little visit, and we shall all be ready
to walk to the Schänzli."

The captain grew very red, and his
moustache bristled.

"I—I—I"—he began to stammer with
impatience—"I cannot go away directly.
I have not yet had a word with the dear

little girl. Ma foi, madame, I cannot leave her yet."

He turned from her abruptly, and went down the stairs as fast as he could.

But the mistress of the "Red Glove" was a match for him.

"Monsieur, monsieur!" she called out; "will monsieur have the kindness to wait a moment?" Then, as he stood still, she hurried down and stood beside him on the landing. "I have something to say, mon·sieur"—she meant to smile, but her narrow lips made the effort more like a grin—"something that cannot be called out from storey to storey. Monsieur knows better than I do; he is more experienced in such matters;" she fixed her cunning eyes on his face; "but I know what girls are, and I fancy monsieur will not make the most of his advantages."

"Eh?—what? What is the meaning of

your words ? I do not know much about
girls," he said, with an abashed look which
almost upset her gravity.

" Well, monsieur, I can explain myself,
I hope, without giving you offence. If 1
were a handsome officer, and went courting,
I should leave the girl to think a little over
the honour I had done her by saluting
her."   Then, unable to keep in her laughter
at his look of bewilderment : " Well, then,
if monsieur takes my advice—and I do know
something about girls—it is wiser, as I said
before, to leave Marie a bit to dream over
that kiss, till she begins to want another.
Aha ! "

The captain was not convinced ; he felt
like a dog robbed of a bone.

" I have left my hat in the parlour," he
said.

" A hundred pardons, monsieur, but I
took the liberty."

And she presented him with his hat, which she had kept hidden behind her.

Loigerot was very angry, he gulped down a strong word with difficulty. "I shall meet you as you come from vespers, madame," he said stiffly. "I have the pleasure of saying au revoir."

When Madame Bobineau had let her lodger out, and had closed the door after him, she grinned. "What a besotted fool the man is!" she said; then she unlocked a side door that led from the passage into the shop, and, crossing it noiselessly, she peeped over the top of the green blind into the parlour.

Marie sat where they had left her, pale and still. Her arms hung down straight beside her, her head was bent forward, but there was an absolute absence of all expression on her face.

Now that Madame Bobineau had got her

own way, she felt some compassion for her
cousin.

"Poor child!" she said.   "I do not
wonder; he is clumsy and ugly, and he has
no manners.   But what will you?   The
bitterest of medicines is sure to be a tonic.
Bah! why am I so silly? In six months'
time she will have grown fond of her little
ball of a captain."

Then she stole cautiously back to the
passage, and retreated to the kitchen.   She
resolved to leave Marie and her sorrow in
peace until dinner-time, and she also determined that the dinner should be appetising
and abundant, even if her own supper
suffered in consequence.

The old glover felt in an excellent
humour.   It is surprising how benevolent
we become when we have our own way.

CHAPTER II.

ON THE TERRACE OF THE SCHÄNZLI.

" To swallow gudgeons ere they're catched,
    And count their chickens ere they're hatched."
                                    HUDIBRAS.

SUNDAY's storm has cleared the air, and
although yesterday was gray and unde-
cided, the sun has asserted himself again
on this Tuesday morning, and gives every
promise of a fine evening.

Rudolf Engemann tells himself this as
he looks at some placards on the piers of
the arcades in the main street of Berne.
On these is announced a concert at the
Schänzli for this evening. Rudolf had seen

this announcement last night on his return from Bâle, where he had to go yesterday on business for the bank, and he then determined to get tickets for the entertainment, and to offer one to Madame Carouge. Now he goes into the shop indicated on the placards, and purchases two tickets.

Going out again he meets the captain bent on a similar errand, but Rudolf does not care to stop and chat with him, he contents himself with a nod, and hurries on to breakfast at the Hôtel Beauregard.

The captain stands on the doorstep of the shop and looks after him, balancing himself alternately on his toes and heels. He nods his head several times, then he shakes it, finally his hands explore his capacious pockets and stay in them.

"Poor devil! he is hard hit. But he will not enjoy life as I shall with my girl-wife. Madame is certainly a fine woman, but the difference of age is on the wrong side," he smiles. "Aha! I shall have my little duck to myself this evening. I have not seen much of her yet; I must get the wedding fixed without delay—delays are dangerous."

He looks radiant, he almost smacks his lips as he turns to the counter and asks for three tickets.

"I suppose they have them given to them at the hotels," he says, as he takes them.

"Yes, monsieur."

"Engemann has wasted his money," the captain thinks, "but still he is on the right track. Yes, yes, it is undoubtedly an attention he should pay to the widow. I do not understand his absence from the dinner-table yesterday; it did not look well. One cannot be too attentive under such circumstances; ma foi," he gives his pocket a slap as he places the tickets inside it; "it was hard work at first with Marie, but I fancy it will be plain sailing now. Those kisses were very pleasant; next time I shall stop midway on those rosy lips."

He smacks his lips this time and goes off to prosecute the morning walk which gives him such a keen appetite for breakfast. He feels impatient for the evening. The storm had upset his plans on Sunday, and the thunder gave Marie such a headache that she went home to bed at a very early hour. He had seen her yesterday, but Madame Webern had come into the "Red Glove" for a gossip, and he could only get a few words with his shy, sweet betrothed. He took her some fresh flowers, and she thanked him; and then she listened while he told her of all she would see and hear at the Schänzli; but she had been very timid and silent. Madame Bobineau had whispered to him

that girls in love were always silent, and
that in his absence Marie talked of him;
but the captain was not quite content. It
seemed to him, however, that this evening
must reward him for the self-denial he
had been forced to exercise.

The day seemed long, and he was disap
pointed in his hope of a talk with Madame
Carouge. Yesterday she had been absent
from her parlour, and to-day she seemed
completely absorbed as she bent over her
desk, and the captain found it impossible
to conquer the awe with which the handsome widow had lately inspired him. She
seemed to him so different to other women,
and he regarded Rudolf Engemann with
increased admiration as the possessor of this
beautiful creature's affections. He dined
alone to-day so as to start in good time
for the Schänzli, and he did not see whether
Engemann went to the widow's parlour.

Dinner over, Captain Loigerot set his hat a little on one side, and then rolled, in his leisurely fashion, into the street which farther on called itself the Spitalgasse.

At the "Red Glove" Madame Bobineau was in anxious expectation; both she and Marie were ready to start, and the old woman feared if the waiting were prolonged Marie would break down.   Just now she had begun to sob, only two sobs came, and then clasping her hands, the girl forced herself to be still.

Madame Bobineau's unusual kindness since Sunday had unnerved Marie.   She suspected that it was by Madame Bobineau's invitation that Madame Webern had come in yesterday evening just before the captain appeared, so that there had been no opportunity for private conversation, and Marie had overheard the old woman request Monsieur Loigerot to keep away during business hours on Tuesdays, lest he should be in the way of her customers. Now, when the old woman came up to her and kissed her on both cheeks, she had a hard struggle to keep in her tears.

"That's a good girl," said Madame Bobineau; "a very good girl, you have done very well"— she took a huge pinch of snuff and patted Marie's shoulder— "and you are going to be so happy, dear child. I lay awake quite a long time last night thinking of your happiness. Behave well to your husband, and he'll give you rings and brooches and silk gowns, and I don't know what besides—perhaps some Brussels lace. Mon Dieu! Marie, think of that."

"Do not, madame," said Marie. "Do not torment me."

They were waiting in the shop, and madame had not put up the shutters lest she should lose the chance of a late customer.

Just then the captain opened the door and came in smiling and bowing first to Marie and then to the old woman.

"Ah, monsieur, you are in good time."

The captain nodded to her, and going up to Marie he took her hand, bent over it, and kissed it.

The girl twitched her hand away with an involuntary movement of disgust.

"Marie," said Madame Bobineau, "run and fetch my blue shawl, there's a good girl, it must be time to start."

The girl hurried away upstairs, and Madame Bobineau patted the captain's arm.

"Monsieur does not mind her odd ways, does he?" she said in her oiliest tones. "No, no, he is too wise ; she is only shy ; girls are all a little shy at first with their lovers ; but believe me, monsieur, it soon goes off. Men have only got to be patient. Why, when first I began to take snuff I used to sneeze, and now"—she stopped and took a hug pinch—"take no notice, Monsieur le Capitaine, and she'll soon get used to you."

The captain fidgeted. He felt that Madame Bobineau's simile was superfluous, but his good-nature triumphed.

"No doubt you are right, madame. I must restrain my—my ardour ; she is shy, pretty little angel, and I like her for it. But—how soon do you think she will get used to me ? "

"Ah, monsieur cannot think how fond the child really is of him, how she talks of him ! What a thing it is to be handsome and amiable ! Mon Dieu ! monsieur will be a happy man."

The captain's eyes glistened, but Marie came in with the shawl before his delight had uttered itself. He gave the girl a loving look as he took the shawl from her and put it over his arm.

"Now, are we ready ? " he said. "We shall find a carriage round the corner, ladies. I consider that the walk would be too fatiguing, we shall have to walk up and down a good deal when we get to the gardens."

He offered one arm to Marie and the other to Madame Bobineau; and they started for the Schänzli.

The carriage set them down near the top of the steep hill, and they walked up through a plantation till they reached the terrace of the Schänzli gardens.

There were plenty of gay and merry groups already on the terrace. The band was playing a waltz of Chopin's; people sat at little tables ranged along the terrace, or walked up and down, stopping, now and then, to chat as friends met one another; or to gaze over the terrace-railing at the picturesque view of the town; or at the distant range of grand snow giants now scarcely veiled by the clouds.

But the gazers were not so numerous as the promenaders were, and most of the former were evidently strangers to Berne, for those who sat at the little tables sipping lemonade and syrups were diligently studying a huge chart of the mountains, which was passed from one table to another.

Many of the travellers did not seem to care about the chart; they were bent on drinking in the beauty of the scene; as they paced slowly up and down they did not trouble themselves to identify the mountains one from another.

Up the side of the steep hill on which the terrace stood, were vine-clad houses, bowered among trees and glowing flowers; far below them the swift Aar rushed on between its fringes of slender poplars, while above, on the opposite side of this green valley, lay the picturesque houses of Berne, with the dark Münster rising from among

them against a background of green and
purple hills. Far away, stretching right
and left across the horizon, was the mag-
nificent range of snow mountains.

Marie stood still ; she felt spelled with
delight as she gazed on the lovely scene.
She forgot the captain and her sorrow—
everything but the picture before her. A
delicious breeze, that seemed to come straight
from the snow mountains, cooled her flushed
cheeks and blew her brown hair into her
soft, gray eyes. As she looked away from
the view to the wood behind the terrace,
she saw couples seated here and there on
benches under the trees. Two figures,
seated further off than the rest, were indistinct in the increasing gloom. Marie
said to herself, "Some of these people are,
perhaps, happy lovers."

And then a strange feeling came at her
heart, a sort of strangling sensation, and she
looked quickly at her companions.

"I think half the town is here," Madame Bobineau was saying.

"Yes, yes, I think so," the captain answered. "Aha, madame, they have come here to see my happiness. Ha! ha! ha!" Then he turned to Marie. "Is it not all pretty, mademoiselle? And the mountains are just in the right place. I call that a coup de théâtre. Eh, Mademoiselle Marie?"

"It is very beautiful, monsieur," the girl answered sadly. To herself she said: "The mountains will soon fade out of sight, and then all will be gloom like my life—I have done with sunshine."

The glamour of the scene around her had at once vanished when she heard the captain's voice. She belonged to him now, and she felt like a slave.

Just then some one came hurrying across to them out of the darkness under the trees. It was Madame Riesen.

"Good evening, monsieur and madame. Good evening to you, Mademoiselle Marie. Have you met Lorenz, I wonder?" She tried to smile, but she was evidently vexed. As she looked at Marie, she saw that her hand was resting on the captain's arm. "I want you to tell me something," she whispered to Madame Bobineau. "Can you spare me a moment?"

Madame Bobineau took her hand from Captain Loigerot's arm, and stood still beside the clock-maker's wife.

"Is it true that the captain is going to marry that charming little Marie?" she said, in an unbelieving voice, and she nodded towards Loigerot and his companion, as they walked on together in advance.

"Why should it not be true?"

Madame Bobineau was so indignant at her gossip's tone that she did not turn to see how quickly the captain was moving forward.

Loigerot seemed to himself to be treading on air. He had at last got Marie alone without her watchful cousin, and he felt triumphantly happy. He was trying to get free of Madame Bobineau. As he walked on, he was constantly receiving bows and greetings from his acquaintance, and he longed to announce his triumph, to say to his friends, "This charming girl has accepted me as a husband, congratulate me."

"Is mademoiselle amused?" he puffed out.

"Yes, monsieur." To herself Marie said: "At least, I should be amused if I were free. If I could only get rid of you, it would be delightful."

The captain stopped to speak to a fat old gentleman, whose straw hat almost swept the ground as he took it off and bowed to Marie.

The girl's eyes met this old fellow's leer of admiration, and she longed to run away from her companion. She felt a sickening sense of degradation. Every moment seemed to be adding publicity to her engagement, and to be making it more real to her. She looked desperately behind her; Madame Bobineau was whispering up into the ear of her tall companion.

"What are you doing here alone?" she was asking her. For the clock-maker's wife had begun to put troublesome questions.

"Ah!"—Madame Riesen drew herself up—"that is what I ask myself. When I agreed to come to-night for the sake of pleasing our gay widow, I imagined she would be satisfied with Monsieur Engemann's attentions. I assure you I was walking quietly with Lorenz enjoying myself—we had left the pair of lovers seated under a tree—and all at once I looked round to point out something to him, and he was gone."

"Gone back to the widow, no doubt. Why did you not go and look for him? Were you afraid of being in the way?" the old glover said in a pitying voice.

Madame Riesen shrugged her shoulders for answer. She pointed to the couple in front.

"That is a settled affair, then?"

Madame Bobineau nodded her head repeatedly.

"Yes, yes, my good friend, quite settled. You do not think, do you, that I should permit Marie to walk arm-in-arm with a man unless he had engaged to marry her— no." She took a huge pinch of snuff. "Marie is a very lucky girl. Captain Loigerot is a man of property, and is in every way a desirable match."

"Desirable in that way, no doubt; but, my friend, as I said just now, he is far too old for the girl." Madame Riesen felt so

convinced that her husband had stolen back
to the widow that it was a relief to be able
to soften her own vexation by tormenting
her old gossip. "He would be better suited
to me than to pretty little Marie. Stupid,
pompous old fellow, what a wretched life
hers will be! Poor child, I pity her!"

"Poor child, indeed! She needs no
pity; you are mistaken, my good friend;
they are as fond as turtle-doves. You have
no notion how much she likes him. But
now tell me something. Did the other
lovers settle the matter on Sunday?"

This was a question that sorely puzzled
the clock-maker and his wife. Madame
Riesen had reproached her husband for
his interference, which she affirmed had
disturbed the natural course of events
between the lovers, while he stoutly main-
tained that the widow was only amusing
herself, and had no real affection for the

young fellow. But the clock-maker's wife
was not going to repeat this, she felt that
she must keep up with Madame Bobineau
her reputation for superior information.

"I fancy they understand each other;
but"—she put her finger to her pale lips—
"our beautiful friend is reserved, you know.
Monsieur Engemann went off to Bâle
yesterday for the whole day. Poor thing!
I pitied her. It seemed rather unloverlike,
I must say."

"Perhaps he had to go on business," said
Madame Bobineau. "By-the-way, I expected to hear you had all been caught in
the storm on Sunday."

"Yes, we got a little of it; we had
counted on a walk in the pine-wood,
that of course was impossible; we had a
good dinner at the Freienhof and stayed
there till the storm cleared off; this rather
spoiled sport for the lovers."

Madame Bobineau looked slyly out of her narrow eyes.

"I dare say your husband put in a word or two and helped the storm," she said, innocently.

Madame Riesen tossed her head like an impatient horse.

"Not at all; it was not that. Of course Lorenz and I too had words to say; but the storm drove every one under shelter, and very soon the room at the Freienhof filled with strangers, and a tête-à-tête became impossible."

"Ah!" said Madame Bobineau. "Well, then I suppose there will soon be a gay wedding at the Beauregard."

She had quickened her pace till she and Madame Riesen came abreast of the captain and Marie.

"Monsieur le Capitaine will be glad to hear it is all right," the old woman said, "between Monsieur Engemann and our beautiful widow. Here is Madame Riesen, who wishes to offer her congratulations to you on your engagement."

" With all possible pleasure, monsieur, and may I say monsieur has chosen a charming bride. Mademoiselle Marie, you must permit me to wish you every happiness ; " she bent forward and kissed the girl.

Marie was taken by surprise ; she blushed with anger and shame. It had been easier than she had expected to accept the captain as a lover ; but she had not guessed that she should be made to suffer this public exhibition, for it seemed to her that he was showing her off to all the world with smiling triumph as his property.

" It is unbearable," she thought, keeping back her tears with difficulty. " If I could only get home and be by myself ! Perhaps if I ask him he will take me away ; he is a kind man, I am sure of it."

"Madame," the captain was saying, pompously, to the clock-maker's wife, "I trust that the enjoyment of Sunday came up to your—your expectations."

"Yes—yes—certainly, monsieur"—the poor woman would not confess that her husband had been as sulky as a bear, and that the rain had damaged the new mantle she had put on for the excursion—"though, of course, the storm upset our evening as it upset monsieur's, I fancy."

"Madame"—he gave what he meant to be a most loving glance at Marie—"I was in such bliss last Sunday evening, that the weather was indifferent to me—completely indifferent ; I had intended to spend it here, but I was supremely happy somewhere else. Ladies"—he gave a bow which began with Marie and ended with

Madame Bobineau—" you will permit me to offer you some ices. Farther on we shall find a vacant table near the music. Mademoiselle, I observe, likes music."

He pressed Marie's hand with his arm, and looked up lovingly in her face.

Marie bowed. At least when they sat down he must let go her hand, and she thought when they rose again it would be possible to avoid this dreadful walking up and down with him.

She began to think out a means of escape.

CHAPTER III.

STILL ON THE TERRACE.

" Sigh no more, ladies, sigh no more,
Men were deceivers ever ;
One foot in sea, and one on shore,
To one thing constant never ;
Then sigh not so,
But let them go."

SHAKESPEARE.

LENOIR, the hair-dresser, came bustling up
to the spot where Captain Loigerot and
his companions had been standing. He
had seen them, but he had not chosen to
come forward and offer his congratulations.
He considered himself ill-used. Madame
Bobineau had not been open with him.
He had been a good friend to her—a friend,

he thought, such as few persons possessed; he had not forgotten some trifling civilities she had shown him when he was a lad, and in return for these he had written to Bâle to tell her when the business at the "Red Glove" was offered for sale, and he had arranged and facilitated matters for her. He had certainly accepted a commission from the outgoer for having procured him a tenant—but that was all in the way of business; and he considered that Madame Bobineau should have taken him into her confidence before she chose a husband for Marie, or at least after the affair was arranged with the captain.

"There has been something more in it than meets the eye," he thought, as he looked on to where the three ladies were seated with the captain at one of the little tables near the edge of the terrace. "I'll wager that our widow had a hand in it.

Ah, what a woman that is!" he nodded approvingly. Lenoir's father had been French, and it seemed to him that the widow's tactics in this affair justified her nationality, supposing that she had been really afraid of Marie's attractions in respect to Monsieur Engemann. "I can hardly think that of Engemann," he said; "no man would choose spring fruit, however blooming, before a luscious peach."

The little hair-dresser looked more like a tomtit than ever, as he walked along, his head set perkily on one side, and his black eyes glittering keenly in large dark rings that circled them. All at once his beaky nose and his thin pointed chin quivered with excitement. He had suddenly remembered the encounter at the bear-pit; he threw out his hand as if to catch the idea that presented itself.

"Aha," he said, "and I told madame

about it, and I remember that she was so extra languid and indifferent, I fancied at the time that her manner was put on ; now I am sure it was. My friend Lenoir, you were right; it is not so long ago, and now Madame Riesen tells me that the widow is certainly going to marry that fair-haired giant, who had his hair cut yesterday in Fribourg—a mere passage-place between Berne and other cities. Pouf! the Goth, as if fashion of any kind could be found in Fribourg."

He rubbed his hands together and walked on the toes of his polished boots, for his costume this evening was very elaborate. " It seems to me that after all the jolly captain is in my debt. I may have been the means of providing the little Marie with a husband. Yes, yes, my friend, it was probably your news that you had seen Marie and young Engemann together that roused the widow's jealousy, and set her on to make this marriage.   The proof will be to see the two couples meet.   I must not miss that meeting; it gives me an interest, it is something to look out for, and it must happen sooner or later, unless Madame Carouge has already left the gardens; she looked tired enough just now."

He had met Madame Carouge and Rudolf Engemann near the entrance, but he had avoided them.   Now he determined to go in search of the lovers, and to witness their probable meeting with the captain and Marie.

"If they are all on the terrace together they must meet," he thought, and he chuckled.   He felt sure "the young giant," as he called Rudolf, would feel awkward between the the two women.   Going on toward the music platform he overtook the clock-maker.

"Good evening, my friend," said Lenoir, "you seem dull. Are you looking for Madame Riesen? I can tell you where she is."

"Thank you, Lenoir, you are very kind." Riesen was anxious to get rid of the little hair-dresser, and he was also trying to keep out of the way of his wife. "I left her not long ago. I have promised to seek out Madame Carouge."

"Come along with me, then," Lenoir said, "I fancy we shall find them on beyond there."

If they had looked into the gathering shadows under the trees, they would have seen the widow and Rudolf Engemann seated on a bench at this end of the terrace. The two were really almost in a line with the captain and his party, but the tree under which they were sitting was far back—the whole width of the promenade

was between them and the trio round
the table. Moreover, Madame Carouge
and her companion sat with their backs to
the terrace.

Madame Carouge was very quiet when
she first met Rudolf Engemann this afternoon. The delight of his presence over-
powered every other feeling; but on her
way to the gardens with him and with
the Riesens she had time to reflect that he
had made no apology for his absence on
the previous day, and it had seemed to her
when they parted on Sunday that only a
few words were needed to make them all
in all to each other. Why had he not
come to say those words? To-day he was
polite, devoted even in manner, but she
felt that he had gone back in warmth.

"It is my fault, perhaps," she thought.
"I am still too reserved with him, poor,
dear fellow!"

She roused, and began to talk with much animation of their Sunday's journey, till Rudolf became absorbed in listening to her—she brought it all so vividly before him. They had sat down under the trees.

"It was indeed a perfect day, madame ; but I regret losing that walk in the pine-wood ; though, perhaps, it is better we could not have it ; it seems the more to be desired because it was left undone."

"Do you wish for it still ?" she said softly ; and as he met her eyes, their wonderful languid charm seemed to steal into his soul.

"Do I not ?" he said. "When one has experienced the enjoyment I did on Sunday, one is apt to wish that it would repeat itself."

"That shall be when you please," she said. "I, too, feel that our day was left unfinished."

She looked at him again ; and again he

thought how beautiful she was, and how kind. "Most men by this time would worship such a woman; well, I suppose I am made of ice. Madame," he spoke impulsively, "how good and kind you are ! Will you permit me, then, to go with you again to Thun; and next time we will try to finish our day ?"

To those who sat on the terrace it looked already gloomy under the thickly-planted trees behind it; but there was plenty of light in the spaces between them, and Engemann saw the strong effect of his words on his companion's face. A sudden light filled her eyes, and a flush rose on her cheeks, her bosom rose and fell rapidly; then she looked down on the ground, and began to draw patterns on it with the point of her parasol.

Rudolf started, he felt as if some one had suddenly roused him from a pleasant dream.

" What am I doing ? " he thought. " I do not love this woman ; I must take care——" he paused. " Why do I not love her ? " he asked himself. He moved impatiently ; between him and the glowing, downcast face beside him rose the sweet, innocent eyes of Marie—he turned as if from a spectre ; she was a girl who had flirted, who had no heart, no feeling—— " It is folly, and worse, to think of her." And then the question seemed to utter itself without his will : " Are you quite sure that Madame Bobineau's cousin will marry Captain Loigerot ? "

He had uttered his thoughts aloud, without considering the abruptness of the transition.

Madame Carouge looked at him in astonishment, then she rose and looked imperious, though she tried to speak gently. " Let us go on to the terrace, monsieur,' she said; "perhaps there you may be able to judge for yourself. I heard that Captain Loigerot was to be here this evening; we shall find him probably with little Marie, watching for the sunset."

She felt deeply wounded; and without another look at Rudolf she walked across to the terrace.

CHAPTER IV.

"It is a basilisk unto mine eye,
  Kills me to look on't—let there be no honour
  Where there is beauty; truth, where semblance; love,
  Where there's another man . . . .
  Oh, above measure false!"

Cymbeline.

THEY walked over the grass beneath the trees till they came out on the broad promenade, which, when they arrived at the Schänzli, had been covered with groups of merry people chatting to one another as they paced up and down.

Now it was almost deserted, though a few couples still lingered here and there;·

but these had seemingly come to the
gardens to look into one another's eyes;
and it was surprising, considering the steep
and tiring road they must have climbed,
that they had taken the trouble to come
thus far for such a purpose.

Madame Carouge looked round with
impatience. Not among these sentimental
lovers should she find the captain and
his fiancée. She glanced on to the edge
of the terrace, and she could have stamped
with vexation. It was literally thronged
with people staring across the valley. She
guessed what was happening; she had
never come up here to see the sight, but
she knew very well that all these "idiots,"
as she mentally called them, were waiting
to see the sun set; and as she looked,
she saw that she had yet some time to
wait before they could meet Captain
Loigerot and Marie. No one could be

distinguished in the closely-packed line of people that leaned on the railing of the terrace, and no one would be likely to move out of it till "the after-glow" had faded. So they waited side by side, a little behind the crowd; and as yet the sun had not set.

Presently there was a hush among the spectators. The light clouds that had partly veiled the mountains had floated upward, and hung suspended above the Jungfrau, as if they, too, would gaze on the coming spectacle; they gleamed with golden brilliance as the sun, resting opposite, seemed to look at them from a ridge which glowed darkly purple below him.

All at once he sank behind the ridge, and then high up on the snowy peaks, which seemed almost in heaven, a soft rosy light shone out of the glorious mountains.

Each moment the glow deepened; the lines just now so brilliant in silver light, were first gold and then a dazzling flame colour; the dusky terrace was suddenly illuminated; and the valley, which had been blurred into a uniform tint of olive, revealed once more its nestling buildings and the fringe of trees below, beside the river.

A murmur ran softly along the line of gazers, but their eyes did not stray from the splendid spectacle. It glowed deeper and deeper, and the sky became luminous with golden-edged scarlet clouds. . . .

Then came a sudden change: the rosy flames that seemed to have rushed out of the heart of the snow mountains vanished; purple, or rather gradations of deep, rich-toned colour, spread up from the base of the mountains, aud glowed on the opposite hills, deepening and darkening every moment, not so startling or vivid, perhaps, as " the after-glow " had been, but yet more beautiful in sombre richness of colour.

But the greater part of the crowd did not wait to see this new beauty ; the closely-packed line had already broken up again into groups, that found gossip about their own affairs or scandal about their neighbours far more interesting than the splendid study of colour in the sky and on the mountains.

Rudolf Engemann, however, lingered ; the purple hues were changing every instant, and he stood gazing in an ecstasy of admiration at the wonderful changes on sky and mountains. He could not have defined his delight, but as he bent forward, enjoying it, he forgot Madame Carouge altogether ; he was under a spell, and he felt entranced.

A little way on from where he stood with the widow, was the table from which the

captain and his party had risen to watch the
sunset.   The others had now turned away
from the sight, but Marie went on gazing
at the mountains; she did not see that the
captain was waiting patiently for her.

The purple hue quickly faded away into
a sombre tone that would have been black
if it had been less full of deep colour; this
made the golden sky yet more luminous, and
the pale faint green above, ethereal in its
beauty; and then all gradually became gray.

"Marie, Marie," Madame Bobineau's harsh
voice broke into the girl's enjoyment, "do
you not hear?   Captain Loigerot has twice
offered you his arm, and you keep him waiting and pay no attention."

"Ah!"—the girl started.   "I beg your
pardon, monsieur."

Then, seeing that the captain looked
kindly at her, she turned to him as to a
refuge from the vexed face of her cousin.

" It is nothing, my sweet young lady ;
your pleasure is, and will always be my first
consideration. You — aw — you consider,
then, this sight has been worth coming to
see."

He stood with his legs wide apart, and
his head thrown back, as if he had uttered
a question that it would puzzle her to
answer.

The intense beauty Marie had been enjoying had filled her eyes with tears, but she
could not help smiling into the captain's
broad, bronzed face.

" Yes, indeed, monsieur, thank you," she
said; "I am glad we stayed to see it." Then
she added, for this seemed a good opportunity for getting away : " It is time to go
home, I think."

She said this to him with a little feeling
of triumph, for she felt that the captain
would most likely comply with her wish

even if it went against that of Madame Bobineau.

"Yes, oh yes, we will go if you wish it," he answered, but he looked disappointed.

Marie had spoken a minute too late. Without looking round, she knew that Madame Bobineau was shaking hands with some one, and now the captain looked sharply round as a hand touched his shoulder.

Monsieur Riesen stood beside him, and in front was Monsieur Lenoir. The little hair-dresser was bowing low to Marie and also to Loigerot, with an indescribable mixture of malice and amusement in his bright, restless eyes.

"Permit me to congratulate you, monsieur," said Riesen. Then to Marie, "Mademoiselle, you have my best wishes."

Riesen had a fatherly, protecting air while he spoke, and his wife kept up an accompaniment of "Yes, yes; Lorenz has come

to offer you his congratulations; yes, yes,
that is as it should be."

"It is delightful to see people so well-
matched," said Lenoir, in his jerky, imper-
tinent way; he looked with his head on
one side at Marie and the captain.

Marie felt that she could no longer stand
still to be stared at and congratulated.
"They are all trying to torment me," she
thought. Her cheeks burned. "They must
despise me in their hearts. It is not to be
borne." But she had placed her hand within
the captain's arm, and, as if he suspected her
feelings, he tightened his pressure so that
she could not draw away her hand without
his knowledge.

"Let us walk down to the end of
the terrace," Madame Riesen whispered to
the old woman; "the music is so noisy
here."

"I cannot leave Marie, and we must

soon be going home," Madame Bobineau answered repressively.

"Ta, ta, my dear friend; we have only to lead the way, the others will follow us like sheep."

Madame Riesen knew that her husband would oppose any suggestion she might make, and she was completely weary of the old glover's society. Among the groups now coming up to listen to the music she hoped to shake her off when she had secured a more amusing companion.

"Shall we go this way, and then turn and make for the gate?" said Madame Bobineau to the captain.

Lenoir smiled and chuckled as he heard the suggestion. He knew that Madame Carouge and her lover must be at that end of the terrace, for he had just come in the opposite direction, and he had been looking in vain for the commanding figure of the young Swiss.

Madame Bobineau and her friend walked so completely in front of her that Marie now felt sheltered from notice. She was no longer so shy of the captain in this crowd of strange people.

"It is pleasanter to walk without stopping," she said; "does not monsieur think so?" She smiled at him as she spoke.

"What a little duck!" the captain said to himself. "I believe she is really fond of being alone with me; the old woman was right after all."

"Mademoiselle Marie"—he tugged at his moustache as if to get his words out—"it is as you say; for me it will always be as you say and as you wish. You shall be my rudder, you shall direct my course in all things, for I see that you are wise, as wise as you are beautiful, and—and wisdom is even more rare than beauty in a young lady of your—your years."

He had puffed out his cheeks in uttering this unusually long speech, till Marie could not keep in her laughter ; but she laughed so merrily and pleasantly that the captain took it in good part, and squeezed her hand so tightly and with a look of devotion so ardent that a bright blush rose on her fair face.

There was a rustling of silken skirts close at hand, an exclamation from the captain, and Marie's eyes dilated as she looked on before her. Madame Bobineau was not to be seen, but in front of them stood Madame Carouge holding out her hand to the captain. The girl felt scorched and withered—Monsieur Engemann stood beside the beautiful widow, and the girl met his eyes full of angry scorn.

"Good evening, Captain Loigerot." Madame Carouge looked at Marie as she spoke. "I congratulate you ; this is as

it should be ; it is a pleasure, my dear, to
see your happiness," she added to the girl.
" You have my best wishes."

Marie trembled, but she did not speak.

Engemann bit his lip fiercely. "It is
true, then," he said to himself, "she does
care for this pompous old satyr."

The captain was bowing very low.

" Madame, I thank you a thousand times
—a thousand times, madame. I am a proud
and happy man to-night." He stood on
tiptoe and tried to whisper to the widow,
but his words also reached Engemann.
" My—my rosebud is all that I could wish,
as sweet and loving as she is lovely. And
you, madame," he raised his voice and
looked knowingly at Rudolf, "you, I hope
—are as happy as we are." He glanced
fondly at Marie, but her eyes were bent
on the ground. "Sweet little dove, she
is shy," he thought; "she does not like

to be stared at." "Come, Engemann, have you not a word of congratulation for me and for mademoiselle?"

"I, monsieur!" Engemann looked very stern, but he managed a grim smile. "On the contrary, I have many for you both. I am glad you can be so easily happy."

He said this mockingly, and then he moved on quickly in the opposite direction, with Madame Carouge on his arm. He strode along, frowning heavily as he looked on the ground.

"Well," said Madame Carouge, "are you convinced they are engaged? And Marie is quite content, you see. We did not see the matter as she does, I fancy."

He did not answer.

The widow glanced at him without turning her head, but she did not again venture to intrude into his thoughts; she felt afraid of him in that moment, and her jealousy flamed out in her eyes. It seemed to her that she had been right, he must have cared for this simple-faced child, or he would not be so disturbed by the certainty of her engagement to Captain Loigerot.

Madame Carouge suffered keenly; after all the love she had betrayed to him, he seemed to be slipping away from her. Her passion sought to hold him, and yet her pride kept her restrained. But she loved him too dearly to sacrifice the hope of his love to the indulgence of her pride, and yet not even her absorption in him could teach her how best to approach him now. She walked beside him, silent, with the timid downcast air of a child expecting reproof, until they reached the end of the terrace. Here she stopped.

"Need we walk quite so fast?" she said, and her voice sounded tearful.

Rudolf started out of his reverie. At

that moment when he seemed so indifferent,
he was in reality nearer to Madame Carouge
than he had ever been. As he strode away
from Marie and her captain, he had up-
braided himself for his infatuation; he had
called himself a fool in respect of that
heartless girl, and a brute with regard to
Madame Carouge. He had been cold to
this tender, loving woman for the sake of
a flirt, who had sold herself to a gray-
beard, and who was evidently rejoicing
in the bargain she had made. As he
recalled the laugh he had seen on Marie's
face when they came up to her, and the
captain's amorous glances, Rudolf frowned
once more heavily.

The widow saw the frown and she sighed.

He turned quickly to her. "You must
forgive me, madame; I ought not to have
walked so fast. How thoughtless I am,
thoughtless in every way! I must have

tired you past endurance; forgive me, indeed I have much, very much to ask pardon for."

She gave him a tender, timid smile, there was comfort in his words; but then they might only mean kindness.

" It is no matter; I am not very tired, but I believe I must say good night now. I seem to be sadly unfortunate; I hoped when you asked me to come, that this evening would have given you pleasure also. You, who admire beauty so ardently, I thought would delight in the sunset as much as I did, and instead——" She hesitated.

" It is not your fault that the evening has not given me unmixed pleasure."

He pressed with his other hand the fingers that lay within his arm.

" In some way or other I fear it has given you pain," she said plaintively; but her eyes . hone with joy.

"What a lovely, loving woman! She only cares for what I feel, she does not dwell upon her own feelings," he thought, and his gratitude showed in his eyes, "how little I deserve such goodness!" "No, madame," he said impulsively, "you have been all that is kind and sweet, and I have been cold and ungrateful—my only excuse is, I am not myself this evening, I must ask you to forgive me."

"I?" She gave him one tender glance. "No, no!" she said, "I have nothing to forgive. I only wished to see you happier, and —and——" She hesitated; tender, ardent words were on her tongue, but she checked them; she felt that she was on the edge of her fate, and she wished to prolong these delicious moments. "My dearest wish," she said quietly, "is to make you happy, and I do not think," she added, with a little laugh which was pathetic, for it tried to hide how intensely she felt what she was saying, "I do not think I quite know the way —do I?"

He released her hand from his arm, and then he took it between his own.

" What can I say to such sweetness?" his voice was hoarse but full of feeling. " Will you forgive me all my rudeness, all my coldness?" He bent over her hand and kissed it. "I will indeed try to deserve all this goodness."

Madame Carouge could not speak; this sudden change took away her breath. She felt lifted off the cold, dull earth into that paradise of warm, rosy love which the glowing mountains had awhile ago pictured to her; for a grand spectacle of nature is many-tongued in its messages as it reveals itself to the varied minds that drink in its varied teaching through their eyes.

She looked up suddenly at her com-

panion, but she did not meet his eyes.
He was gazing far off at the purple mass
that girdled in the scene, and made even
the terrace gloomy.

"It will soon be dark," he said gravely.
The sudden glow that had drawn him
towards his companion had died away
already.

She was not thrown back now as she
had been on former occasions by his change
of manner. The spell of his presence
subdued her will, even her sensations, into
union with his; she began to understand
that his manner would always be subject
to change, and she answered him in the
same tone.

"Yes, it is getting dark. I am ready to
go home. Shall we tell Monsieur Riesen
to see after the carriage?"

Engemann bowed, and they went on
along the terrace. She was silent from

joy; at last she knew that he loved her.
Perhaps he had always loved her, and only
the doubt and fear of her own feelings had
clouded her sight with this foolish want
of confidence. That kiss on her hand had
thrilled through her being; it had been the
seal of their love, she thought, and she
emptied her heart of the dark fears it had
harboured, and let in a band of bright
hopes. She sighed softly with almost a
weight of joy.

"Ah! here is Monsieur Riesen," Rudolf
said.

They had come up to the husband and
wife standing in the middle of the promenade which was now almost deserted, for
though the music had only just ceased,
people were rapidly leaving the gardens.

"At last we have found you," cried the
clock-maker's wife coming forward; and the
widow thought her cackling voice seemed

to clash harshly into the delicious silence. "A pair of truants, indeed. But I suppose we must excuse them; eh, Lorenz?"

"Don't be a fool," her husband muttered.

"Will you have the kindness to find the carriage, Monsieur Riesen?" Madame Carouge said to him. "I must go home, I had no idea it was so late."

But the clock-maker felt that this was the last straw, and that he could not carry it. His evening had been altogether hateful to him, and he had been obliged to admit to himself that, after all, his wife had been in the right, and that Engemann was in earnest in his pursuit of the widow; he had not once left her side during the evening, and Riesen had scarcely had a chance of speaking to her. It had been exasperating. He looked at Madame Carouge, and he saw how subdued she was, and how young and happy she looked. He felt very angry.

"Engemann, my good fellow," he said, "I have a weak ankle, and I should be glad to rest it while Pierre puts the horse in if you will go and find him. I told him he might put the carriage up, and enjoy himself in the gardens. Can you find him, do you think?" "Diable!" he said to himself; "that fellow Engemann shall earn his salt somehow."

Engemann was gone before Madame Carouge could speak. To her dismay, she found herself alone with Madame Riesen and her husband.

Part VIII.—The Fly Escapes.

CHAPTER I.

MISSING.

"There's no joy without alloy."
Proverb.
"Life is a series of surprises."
Lord Houghton.

When Rudolf Engemann passed on so scornfully with the widow on his arm, the captain stood still, with his mouth wide open, and a look of displeasure on his broad, full-moon face.

Madame Bobineau, the Riesens, and Lenoir had gone on without noticing the meeting, for Lenoir's eager watching had been at fault. The old woman began to whisper scandal to her friend, and the bird-like barber could not help listening, he was dying to hear what she said.

They had been all too much occupied with themselves to notice what had happened behind them, and, indeed, the flow of people coming up from the end of the terrace, eager to leave the gardens, had by this time completely parted them from the captain and Marie.

"Tonnerre!" Loigerot exclaimed — and between his teeth he uttered some much stronger words—"what does the fellow mean, sneering at a gentleman? And— and he owes me explanation, and he shall give it, or——"

And again a strong word came out, louder than before, as he put his hand to where his sword-hilt should have been.

He had not felt in such a rage since he left the army, and for a minute he forgot where he was; the whole scene became blurred and confused; he longed to have it out with this "insolent clerk," as he termed Engemann.

It has been hinted that Captain Loigerot was in some things rather obtuse; but his position this evening had sharpened his perceptions, and in his sympathy for Marie's sensitiveness he had become quick-sighted; he had not accepted as genuine all the felicitations which had been so lavishly bestowed on him this evening; he had seen ridicule on some of the faces of those who congratulated him; and the malicious sarcasm, as it seemed to him, of Engemann, had stung him keenly. It was evident that this young man, rich in personal advantages, and happy in the love of a beautiful woman, despised him and disbelieved in his good fortune.

For an instant—as he stood bristling with anger from head to foot—Loigerot saw himself as he appeared to Rudolf, middle-aged and doting, fooled into the belief that he was loved for himself. The idea was momentary, but it took his thoughts at once back to Marie. Her hand no longer rested on his arm, and as he looked round quickly and with sudden alarm, he saw that she was not beside him.

"Diable!" he exclaimed, and the colour deepened on his face. "What! Why! In Heaven's name! what has happened? Where is my little dove?"

He looked eagerly about him, but close by was Madame Webern, the pastrycook, and Loigerot was far too old a soldier to let this gossiping woman perceive his discomfiture. He bowed to her, and then he looked toward the table and chairs where they had been sitting. They were empty. Loigerot walked on looking about him, but he tried to hide his discomfiture; for although people were going away fast, still he met an ac-

quaintance here and there. He had been
so triumphant all the evening, he must not
betray to these curious eyes any uneasiness
in his search for Marie.

"Poor little dove!" he said to himself;
he felt in great need of pacifying words.
"Poor little angel! no doubt she was tired,
and she does not like to be stared at. She
has gone after Madame Bobineau. Yes, that
is it; I remember that they were on in
front. She has gone after the old woman;
but it is unwise, she may not easily find
her, and she should not have slipped away
from me. It will soon be dark. I hope
she is not still alone." His face became
pathetic in its expression of alarm. "It is
most foolish, most improper. Well, well, the
sweet child is young and does not know."

It had been arranged between Madame
Bobineau and the captain that they should
all walk home together by the lower bridge,

for Loigerot had not found his drive to the
gardens amusing, perched up beside the
coachman, while the two ladies sat together
behind him.

He stood still, thinking what he should
do now. The ladies were possibly tired of
waiting, they might have gone home alone.
The idea of Marie, perhaps quite alone, or
walking in the dark, with no better pro-
tector than " old Bobineau," as he called
her, filled the captain with alarm, and
quickened his faculties.

He rolled along to the end of the terrace
walk, and then came rapidly back again ;
but he could not see Marie anywhere ; at
length after a keen search among the remaining stragglers, he hurried to the entrance of
the gardens, always looking for the tall figure
in a pale gray gown. But he could not find
either Marie or Madame Bobineau. As he
hastened along, he saw the Riesens and

Madame Carouge standing together, but they did not see him, and he avoided them.

"I am not going," he said to himself, "to let that long-tongued gossip, Madame Riesen, know of my mischance; she shall not hear that Marie ran away from me, I should never hear the last of it," and he hurried on.

Duty was paramount with the captain. He had lost Marie by his own carelessness; it was his place to find her, and he must find her without delay. At first he had been more startled than troubled. After his diligent search through the gardens had failed, he guessed that she had gone away with Madame Bobineau. But although his lack of imagination prevented the captain from conjuring up the doubt and dread which might have affected a more sensitive lover, his common-sense rarely failed him, and by the time he had reached the foot-bridge across the Aar,

without catching up either of the ladies,
he felt puzzled and anxious, unable to
decide what he had best do.

The unaccustomed speed at which he had
walked no doubt added to his disturbance;
but still, even supposing that Madame Bobineau had quitted the gardens when he missed
Marie, he must long ago have overtaken
her. He stood still on the bridge, puffing
and panting; perhaps it would be best to go
back and ask Riesen's help in finding them,
for, after all, they might have sat down to
wait for him in some out-of-the-way corner
of the gardens. But even as he turned back
to carry out this idea, a new and more hope-
ful thought suggested itself. Madame Bobineau had complained of fatigue as they sat
drinking lemonade, and Marie had asked
him to take her home; she, perhaps, was
also tired. Was it not more than likely
that some friend leaving in a carriage had

offered the old woman and her charge seats,
and that Madame Bobineau had carried off
Marie with her?

He shrugged his shoulders. "She is a
wary old bird," he said to himself. "She
arranged that we should all walk home
together, by way of the foot-bridge. I had
counted on this walk with my little girl—
bah! The old woman sees I am secure,
and she no longer studies my wishes. Well,
well, I shall have the marriage fixed a fort-
night hence. I am tired of interference, and
I want my little girl to myself out of the
reach of the old hag."

All this time he was hurrying along by
the short way to the Spitalgasse — he
guessed that he should find Madame Bobineau at home—and this short way was up a
flight of steep steps in the lofty green bank
on which stand the houses and churches of
Berne looking down into the poplar-fringed

Aar. Loigerot's face had become purple
with exertion, and he gasped when he
reached the top of the steps. He took off
his hat and stood still to recover his breath,
for, although it was dusk, the heat still lingered with the strange atmospheric pressure
that threatens storm.

"Pouf!" he gasped; "you forget your
extra weight and your short wind, my
friend Achille, and the years since you
were at the Malakhoff; my wind was right
enough then! Diable! perhaps it is love
that helps to make my heart beat; that
is too amusing, you old dog!" and he
laughed heartily at himself in spite of his
breathless condition. "Well, well," he
wiped his bald head and put on his hat,
"to work again, my friend; it is a hard
end to a day's pleasure, but the reward will
be the sweeter, and the little rogue shall
pay me in kisses. Ah! We will have no
more make-believes; that old mummy shall

not come between us with her precious
advice." He smacked his lips heartily, and
hurried on in his rolling fashion to the " Red
Glove."

The big red sign looked almost scornful
and threatening to the captain as a ray
from the gas lamp glinted on it.

Loigerot knocked twice, but no answer
came. He knocked more loudly a third time.
" Diable !" he said ; " this grows serious :
but I have perhaps arrived first." He
looked up again at the Red Glove. Something in the aspect of the bloated sign made
him shake his clenched fist at it. It seemed
to mock him. He stood still, gazing, his
temper was rising, while his face grew yet
more angry ; at last he turned away. " I
am not going to be made a fool of, and I'll
never be laughed at by an old she-devil of
a glover. She is gorging herself with
supper, no doubt she pretends not to hear."

His sturdy legs were very wide apart as

he stood opening the private door with his pass-key.

"Madame Bobineau! Madame Bobineau!"

He roared and shouted her name downstairs, in the kitchen, upstairs; the shop door was locked, or he would have gone in there. He had lost all self-control, and he even knocked at Engemann's door.

The house was like a grave—dark, silent, and stifling in its atmosphere, for every window had been closely shut by the old glover before she left home.

Loigerot came slowly downstairs, a little ashamed of his excitement; he stood thinking on the mat in the passage.

All at once he opened the door, banged it behind him, and hurrying up the street he turned to the left and soon reached the flight of steps leading down to Marie's lodgings. "She may have come home without

madame," he thought, "and she would perhaps go straight to her lodgings." He had
watched the girl home more than once;
but when he arrived at the door of the
house he had seen her enter, he felt that this
proceeding was open to objection; would
it not be injurious to Marie if any one
saw him at the door of her lodgings?

"I will risk it; it is dark," he said, "and
there are not many people about," and he
knocked.

The door was slowly opened. "Who is
there?" a woman's voice asked.

"Is Mademoiselle Marie Peyrolles at
home?"

The captain could not distinguish anything in the dark passage through the half-
opened door.

"No," and the door began to close.

Loigerot put his foot just within. "I
beg your pardon," he said politely, "but

are you sure of what you say, madame? The young lady may have come in without your knowledge."

"That is not possible," the croaking voice said; "she has no key."

"You are quite sure, madame; some one else may have opened the door for her? Will you have the goodness to go and inquire if Mademoiselle Marie is within?"

There was a pause, then a grunt came from the speaker; the door was closed, and he heard a heavy step going upstairs.

He waited with a smile of relief. "It is all right," he said, "no doubt Madame Bobineau has seen her home, and has then gone off to some of her gossips. Poor little girl, it is horrible to think of her being lodged in such dirty quarters, but we will make all that right before long. Ah! here the woman comes."

The door opened again and he felt
radiant with hope, but the harsh voice jerked
out : " She has not come in ; she is not in
her room," and the door was shut in his
face.

The captain stood looking blankly at
the door. So far he had followed instinct,
and had felt a sort of blundering surprise
at his own cleverness. Now he looked
as clumsy and as helpless as a performing
bear does when he has played out all his
antics. There is nothing to be done in
the bear's case but to repeat his perform-
ance, and the only idea that came to
Captain Loigerot was that he must go back
to the gardens, and begin his search over
again.

" I came by the short way, by the foot-
bridge, as we had settled to come," he
said, with self-reproach, " and they may
have kept to the road and are coming

across by the upper bridge." He tugged
at his moustaches as though seeking his
usual counsel from them. A sudden and
most comforting idea came to his assistance ;
it was evident that Madame Bobineau and
Marie were together, for they were both
missing.

The captain drew a deep breath of relief,
and, holding his head erect, he rolled down
the street, resolved to follow it to its end,
and thus lose no chance of seeing the
fugitives in the event of their being in a
carriage.

"Sapristi !" he muttered ; "it was all the
fault of that idea of walking home. Achille,
when will you learn to be reasonable, and
to remember that you are no longer twenty
years of age, and that little Marie does not
care a centime for walking home with you
in the dark ? She is not taken with your
bright eyes, as some others were years ago.

But—but, ma foi," he nodded complacently, "I caught her several times smiling at me, little dear. When a girl is shy she is the devil for hiding her feelings, but they peep out spite of her caution. Well, well, the shy game will soon be over with her."

He did not walk back as fast as he had come; there were a good many people at this end of the town, and he did not wish to attract observation. When he had turned out of the streets and was on his way to the bridge beneath the railway, he began to meet scattered groups who were returning from the Schänzli. These gradually dispersed themselves into the town by various side turnings, and soon the road was deserted. But there was nothing to be seen of Marie and Madame Bobineau.

"Ciel! where are they?" said the captain between his teeth; "it is most extraordinary."

By this time he had reached the suspension bridge. Lights were twinkling among the houses on the opposite bank, and a murmur of voices came up from the poplar-fringed walk far below beside the river. There was a cold gleam on the water, wholly unlike its usual aspect. The bridge vibrated as the sound of a carriage was heard coming across it : the gas-lamp at this end was lit, and Loigerot stood under it, ready to examine the occupants of the coming vehicle.

As the carriage emerged from the covered bridge and was passing him, a cry was heard from within.

"There is the captain!" was called out. "Captain Loigerot!" And from the box Lenoir joined in the duet between Riesen and Madame Bobineau in the carriage.

Lenoir stopped the coachman; but by the time Loigerot had reached the carriage-door Madame Bobineau had sunk down in a heap on the seat and was shaking with terror. She had seen that the captain was alone. She could not get out a word.

"Here you are at last!" said Loigerot joyfully.

"Where is Mademoiselle Marie?" asked the clock-maker.

"What have you done with the little one?" his wife cried.

"Yes, yes," said Lenoir, with a grin, "we are anxious to know what has happened to mademoiselle."

Madame Carouge did not say a word, but her face looked white in the gloom as she peered out at the captain.

He literally trembled, but he did not speak. He felt devoutly thankful that Madame Riesen kept up an incessant cackle. It gave him time to recover from the shock he had received, and to face the situation

M 2

at all points; for, in addition to the dread of giving food for gossip, natural to a man of his age and circumstances, as he recovered from the alarm of his discovery, he felt keenly that Marie's good character was involved in her disappearance. A sudden inspiration came to him.

"This is amusing," he forced a laugh. "I came to find you, Madame Bobineau. Mademoiselle Marie wants you, and I have something to tell you as we go along. Come, let me take you home. You will not mind a little walk."

He opened the carriage door and let down the steps, then he took the old woman's hand and drew her out of the carriage in such a masterful way that she meekly obeyed.

"But you will be tired, madame," the widow spoke sweetly, for a sudden relief had come to her with the captain's words; just now she had been seized with a horrible fear when she saw Captain Loigerot standing alone under the gas-light.

"Do not wait; go on," said Loigerot.

"Good night!" Madame Carouge said as the carriage rolled away.

"Mon Dieu!" said Madame Bobineau, "how thankful I am! It is such a relief to hear that the dear child is safe. When I saw you alone, monsieur, I nearly fainted. I had sent Lenoir to find you in the gardens, and when he came back without tidings I said to myself, 'Mon Dieu! it is all right; Marie is with the captain, he will take care of her; and, as it is dark, no one will notice my absence; besides, he is almost her husband.' So I came along with Madame Carouge, and——"

"Please to tell me, madame"—the captain's voice was very harsh, and his manner was rude—"what all this means? Where is Marie? What have you done with the little girl? You know very well she is not with me——"

"She is not with you!" the old woman's alarm was too real to be mistaken, and as his frown softened she flew at him, and grasped his arm. "I—I, indeed! what have I done with her! What do you mean, monsieur? I left Marie with you. What have you done with her? Do you venture to tell me you have not taken her home?"

She was in such rage and terror that she shook her fist in his face.

It only wanted a trifle to upset the rest of the captain's self-control.

"Mille diables," he said roughly, "do not be an old fool. I wash my hands of you and Marie too. Do you think I'll marry a girl who runs away by herself in the dark?" and he swore at her roundly.

Madame Bobineau was cowed, and she saw that she must be prudent.

"There is no use in quarrelling," she said. "We can settle that when we have found the naughty girl. But do you mean, monsieur, that you went away, that you left the gardens without her?"

"Confound you! I tell you I missed her suddenly; she—she went away. I thought she had gone to you. I have been to the 'Red Glove,' but she is not there. I have been to her lodging; she is not there," he said, with slow and angry emphasis. "Diable! what am I to think?"

Madame Bobineau stood thinking. She slowly recovered herself. "What does monsieur propose to do?" she said at last, very quietly, for she began to fear that it might be left to her alone to find the lost girl.

"I am going back to the gardens, madame. When I find I have lost my way, I go back to the place I started from. It seems to me possible, I only say possible," he said gravely, "that the poor child felt ill, and she may still be sitting, waiting for me, under the trees at the Schänzli."

He turned away. Before he had gone many steps, he came back to Madame Bobineau.

"You, madame," he puffed out his words sententiously, "had better wait here. There is a bench not far off. You must wait here till I come back. If she passes you will see her; do you understand? We must not let her slip through our fingers."

He rolled rapidly away over the bridge.

"Holy Virgin! he treats me as if I was the dirt under his feet." Madame Bobineau's eyes gleamed with anger. "It must be bed-time. I am tired to death. I will give that hussy a beating to-night if I never give her another; and then I will not lose sight of her again until she is Madame Loigerot."

CHAPTER II.

"The little stars sat one by one
    Each on his golden throne."
                    LORD HOUGHTON.

"No grim thing written or graven
    But grows, if you gaze on it, bright ;
A lark's note rings from the raven,
    And tragedy's robe turns white ;
And shipwrecks drift into haven ;
    And darkness laughs, and is light.

"Grief seems but a vision of madness ;
    Life's key-note peals from above,
With nought of it more of sadness
    Than broods on the heart of a dove :
At sight of you, thought grows gladness,
    And life, thro' love of you, love."
                    SWINBURNE, *Maytime in Midwinter.*

"YOU are not coming with us," Madame Carouge had said to Rudolf Engemann, and there was tender reproach in her eyes.

Engemann pressed her hand and whispered, "I will see you later."

And now, as he stood looking after the carriage as it drove away from the gates of the Schänzli, he felt a strange mixture of relief and perplexity. At last he was free from the spell which had kept him beside the widow ; he was free to think over all that had happened. But there were still several lingerers near the entrance-gates, and he turned back into the gardens, for he wanted to be alone.

He found the walk beside the terrace already deserted, and going a little way across the grass which bordered it, he flung himself on a bench under the trees. Here, at least, he was safe from intrusion ; the trees overhead increased the gloom around him, and he sighed with a pleasant sense of freedom as he leaned back against the tree-trunk to which the bench was fixed, and clasped his hands behind his head.

Engemann had lived very much alone, and he was not quick-witted, and both these causes made it difficult for him to disentangle his thoughts when he was with others. The glow of feeling which he had experienced beside Madame Carouge had created in him a mental disturbance, a sort of chaos, which he longed to set in order.

His first idea was that he had gone too far with her to draw back ; well, so be it, Marie was lost to him, nothing mattered now, he might as well try to make Madame Carouge happy. Then, as the events of the evening passed in review before him, he started up from his seat and began to walk up and down : he frowned, and it was easy to see that he was suffering mentally. But he turned resolutely from the thought of Marie, and seated himself once more on the bench.

" I do not wish to draw back." His thoughts went on to Madame Carouge and her tenderness. "I care quite enough for her—to make her a good husband, and I believe she cares for me. If I can make her happy, that is all that is necessary to such a plain man as I am." Yes, he must speak out to her to-night; but he wished there could have been a longer delay. Though Marie was nothing to him, yet——

"I was a fool to come here," he cried out, "to run the chance of seeing her again. This stillness makes the bitterness still worse. Oh, Marie! can you be false and worldly, when you look as pure and true as an angel might? How is one to believe in anything?" The poor fellow groaned in his anguish. Marie's sweet face rose before him as he had seen it last at the "Red Glove," with that look of pathetic entreaty in her soft gray eyes.

"I will not believe it," he said, "she is true, there has been some terrible mistake; if Marie is deceitful, then no woman can be true."

After this he remained dumb, while a tempest of sorrow swept over him—and then came reaction. Reality asserted itself, reminded him of Marie smiling in the captain's face and blushing with pleasure at his admiration.

" Good heavens ! " the young fellow said furiously, " how could she bear it ? The odious old baboon."

It was easier now to go back to Madame Carouge. Yes, he had gone too far to delay ; his attentions had perhaps compromised her, he must marry her.

And then his lower nature came to help him, called up the image of the beautiful woman who had shown him such favours and revealed sweet possibilities of love in her deep passionate eyes. Then, too, she could remove all anxiety from his life ;

she could give him ease and comfort, the means of travelling—a wish so near his heart that he let his thoughts go out to it gladly, as to an escape from the miserable feelings which he knew would return.

All at once he thought he heard a voice among the trees. Rudolf listened, but all was again silent. Overhead, the stars were beginning to show themselves, large and luminous, shining with a pure, peaceful light that calmed him. He sat gazing at them, and he felt quieter, less bitter toward Marie.

"I do not know why I call the poor child false," he said. "I have never asked for her love; I have never even said a word of love to her. Ah, but," he said impetuously, "words were not needed. I did not hide what I felt for her, and she—well, her eyes told me more than she knew—if they spoke truly."

He got up again and paced up and down the grass, angry with his own weakness ; he knew that he had himself recalled the temptation. The only safety would be in putting a barrier between himself and his love for Marie.

" What am I about ? " his thoughts went on. " I have no right even to think of Marie, I belong to another woman. What I have to do is to marry that woman and make her happy." He set his teeth defiantly, and then he laughed. " One impression effaces another," he said. " I suppose people will say I am a very lucky fellow. Well, perhaps I am. She is rich and beautiful and she loves me. I dare say I shall soon forget this evening, or think of it as a foolish dream. . . . There ! it is done with—I am due at the Hôtel Beauregard, I am going to be very happy, I have played the fool long enough this evening."

He said this sturdily enough, but he did not at once turn towards the entrance-gate. He again paced up and down, striving for calm and for relief from the bitterness which made the duty he had set himself so distasteful.

"I should have stayed with Madame Carouge," he said angrily, "and then she would have kept me fascinated, and left me no time to think in. Well, I will marry her as soon as she likes, and then all this folly will pass out of remembrance."

But still he kept pacing up and down.

"What is that?" he stopped. "Is any one in there?" he called out. He peered in among the trees. There was certainly a noise; it sounded like a person sobbing. He stood still listening with strained ears. "Ah," he said;—a louder sob reached him; he turned into the darkness and made his way under the trees.

As he advanced he made out a figure on a seat placed against the outside fence; it was a woman, her light gown showed dimly in the gloom. His steps sounded on the twigs and dead leaves, and at the noise the figure raised its head—the sobbing ceased.

" It is a woman in trouble," Engemann said. " Poor soul !—but she will get locked in. I will tell her she must not stay here."

By this time he had reached the seat, and he felt puzzled how to act. The woman kept her head turned away, as if she thought this would shield her from discovery ; and indeed it was too dark to see her face, the trees formed so thick a canopy overhead.

Engemann bent down.

" Madame," he said gently, " I beg your pardon. You are perhaps a stranger, and you do not know that the gardens will soon be closed for the night."

The figure gave a sudden start, but there was no answer, and he waited. He began to distinguish better as his eyes accustomed themselves to the gloom, and he saw that the woman clasped her fingers tightly together.

"You are in trouble." Engemann felt strangely moved by this deep sorrow before him. "Can I be of use to you?"

"Please go away—you cannot help me," came in a broken, disguised voice.

But he recognised it. The shock of his surprise struck him dumb. He stood thrilled with strong emotion, unable to believe that he had really heard Marie's voice.

"What does this mean?" he said at last; then, stooping, he took hold of her arm, drew her gently up from the seat, and far too much moved to care for anything but certainty, he hurried her out of the shadow of the trees to the open space, where it was lighter. Then, as he held her by both hands, the better light showed him her pale, tear-stained face, which she sought vainly to hide from his gaze.

"Mademoiselle Peyrolles," he said severely, " what does this mean ? Why are you here alone ? Where is Captain Loigerot ?"

As he said the name he let go her hands, and they fell straight beside her.

" I do not know where he is ; I do not care. Please go away, monsieur. I wish to be alone."

She spoke sullenly, and turned to go back among the trees.

"You cannot stay here, mademoiselle, it is against the rules of the place," he said. " I will take you out of the gardens, and then I will see you safely home."

"I have no home," she said, in the same sullen voice.

Then she ran back among the trees, and he heard that she was sobbing again.

Engemann stood for a moment irresolute; then he went after her.

Marie had not gone far; he found her leaning against a tree, sobbing and quivering with anguish, for indeed it seemed to her that she had become an outcast; it did not signify what happened to her now.

Her distress softened him. "Poor child," he said gently, "you have, I suppose, lost your friends. You had better go home at once. Or shall I"—he could hardly get the words out—"shall I go and find Captain Loigerot and Madame Bobineau and send them to you? I will do this if you prefer it."

She turned to him and held out her hands beseechingly.

"No, no, for pity's sake, monsieur, do not —do not tell them where I am. I do not want to see either of them again."

A sudden glow of hope spread over Engemann.

" Marie"—he caught her hands passionately in his—"what do you mean ? Which
is the truth ? Are you the girl I saw just
now smiling on the captain's arm ? or are
you really feeling this sorrow ? Which is
your true self ? What has changed you in
this short time ? "

Marie drew her hands away, but she
checked her tears.

" I have not changed, monsieur ; indeed
I always try to be true," she said, in a
broken voice.

" Then why did you promise yourself to
Captain Loigerot ? "

Marie looked up at him in surprise ; he
had forgotten everything but her presence ;
but she remembered quite well that he was
engaged to marry Madame Carouge, and
that she must not betray her feelings to
him.

" What else could I do, monsieur ?

Madame Bobineau had arranged it all, she is my guardian," she said quietly; " what could I do?"

"Then you did not care for the captain ?"

She longed to say "Yes"—this would end his questioning—but she could not.

"No, monsieur, I was very unhappy."

"And yet you agreed to marry him. Oh, Marie!" he went on passionately, "you knew — you must have seen that I loved you—" She started violently.—" And just because that old man is rich you agreed to marry him without giving me a chance."

"You—loved—me!" broke from her in tones of wonder. She hesitated; then she raised her eyes to his. "Are you sure, monsieur ?" she said sadly. "I was told you loved some one else, and then——"

"And then ?"

He had taken her hand again.

" And then nothing seemed to signify," the poor child said. Her face was hot with shame, though she knew the darkness hid it.

" You love me then, darling?" She looked at him timidly, and he did not wait for words. "Darling Marie !" he whispered.

Marie was greatly frightened when she felt his arm round her waist, but she was very happy too. That strong arm was such a safe shield and resting-place ; all trouble seemed to melt away at the touch of it.

" Darling Marie," he repeated, "my sweet one !" and he kissed her.

CHAPTER III.

THE CAPTAIN LEARNS THE TRUTH.

" The best-laid schemes o' mice and men
        Gang aft a-gley ;
And leave us no't but grief and pain
        For promised joy."
                                BURNS.

" Any man may commit a mistake, but none but a
fool will continue in it."—CICERO.

" AN irritable bachelor " is a common
saying ; but the fact that " a single man,"
as he is called, has no one with whom to
share his troubles, ought to excuse the un-
willingness with which he submits his back
to any burden laid on it. Perhaps, too,
having no other legitimate back on which

to lay the blame of disasters, he has a habit of bestowing blame freely in all directions.

It is certain that by the time Captain Loigerot had reached the steep approach to the Schänzli he had considerably eased his mind by the amount of abuse mingled with some unsavoury epithets, which, as he went aloug, he bestowed on Madame Bobineau.

"It is indecent behaviour," he said, savagely, at last pulling himself up, and setting his hat firmly ; " there is no other word for the conduct of an old woman who leaves a girl to run about alone in the dark. Tonnerre ! what would have become of little Marie's character if I had not had presence of mind ? Ah, that is a quality, Achille, that one makes acquaintance with when one comes suddenly on an ambush or a masked battery. Ma foi ! when I remember—— Well, well, I shall

keep the dear girl amused with my stories
one of these days; though, indeed, I—I am
not going to forgive her at once. No, no;
she shall ask me to take pity on her. To
run about alone in the dark! Bon Dieu! But
then if the little rascal smiles at me with
her sweet eyes and mouth, it will be all
over with me in a moment, so take care,
Achille; you must keep a steady hand and
your eyes wide open—— Hallo! stop!
Who the devil—— Why, Marie!"

While he was absorbed in these reflec-
tions he had nearly rolled against Engemann, who came rapidly down the road with
Marie on his arm. " Sapristi ! " he exclaimed
when he saw who they were. "What have
you been doing with mademoiselle, Monsieur Engemann ? "

Then he stood, choked and silenced by
his anger and surprise. But Marie snatched
quickly at his right hand, and in spite

of his resistance Engemann seized on the other.

"Pardon me, monsieur," Marie said.

"Monsieur," said Engemann, "you have been badly used, and it has been my fault——"

"No, no, monsieur," Marie interrupted, "it was my fault; I was much the worst. You have been deceived. I — I cannot marry you, monsieur."

"Deceived! Cannot marry me! What nonsense are you talking? What have you done?" The captain roared as he pulled his hands roughly away; he stood gasping for breath, his legs spread apart like a large inverted V. He looked so stern that the girl's voice trembled.

"I mean, monsieur, that you have been deceived by my cousin."

"Deceived!" he puffed out angrily; "it is you who are deceived, mademoiselle;

you have promised yourself to me with the consent of your guardian, and you are not of age ; therefore you cannot take back that promise."

" Monsieur," Marie cried, " listen ; oh ! do please listen. I have———"

Loigerot backed away from her out-stretched hand. " Do not touch me," he said bitterly. " You are a heartless girl."

But Marie clasped both hands round his arm. She did not feel shy of him now ; for, although he might perhaps part her from her lover, something told her he would not compel her to marry him if he knew that she loved Monsieur Engemann.

" Monsieur " — she looked frankly at him—" you are very angry with me now, and I do not wonder ; but, indeed, monsieur, you should have been angry with me when I said I would marry you. It was wicked of me when I did not care for you."

Loigerot turned away his head. It was much lighter out here on the road than it had been under the trees in the Schänzli, and Marie saw that he had turned a deep red.

"Monsieur," she went on, "be pitiful; do not judge me too hardly; and—and, monsieur, surely you cannot care for a girl who does not love you—who never could love you."

"Then why did you lie? Why did you consent to marry me, you little deceiver?"

He did not trust himself to look at her, and he spoke in a rude, blustering voice over his shoulder.

"It was Madame Bobineau," Engemann began.

Marie looked at her lover.

"Please to go a little back?" she said timidly; the girl began to feel that she had greatly wronged this good, kind man by her weakness. Love and Captain

Loigerot had seemed incompatible; but
she now felt that she had misjudged
him, that she had been altogether selfish
in regard to him. " Monsieur," she clasped
her hands and looked earnestly in his face,
" please listen to me : I will tell you the
simple truth. I have been a thoughtless
girl—heartless, too, perhaps ; but indeed I
did not mean to be. I thought I was doing
right. Madame Bobineau said you wanted
to marry me, and she said she would take
away my character and tell every one I had
behaved badly, unless I obeyed her ; she said
if I did not consent to marry you she would
give me up, and that no one else would
employ me. I am friendless, monsieur, and
I was miserable ; I did not know what to
do, and so I said 'Yes.' I have been very
wrong and foolish, monsieur ; but—but now
I should be wicked if I were to marry you."

Something in the last words struck the

captain. Engemann's silence had quieted his first suspicions, he turned round and looked at Marie.

"What do you mean?" he said crossly; very crossly indeed, for the sight of her fair imploring face made his disappointment yet keener. "Do you mean, by chance, that you had a fancy for Monsieur Engemann, eh, you pretty little jilt?"

Marie hung her head, and made no answer.

"Did Madame Bobineau know this?" he said savagely.

Marie's courage was nearly gone. His rude manner frightened her. She wished she had not asked her lover to go away.

"Madame Bobineau told me that—that I cared for Monsieur Engemann," she said; "but I—I never knew he cared for me till—till just now."

Loigerot swore loudly and violently, and

Marie drew back in alarm. Engemann had been burning with impatience, at this he came forward and stood beside her.

"Monsieur, you must not be angry with Mademoiselle Marie. You must please listen to me. I have been a blind fool, and I have caused much of this trouble. Instead of judging for myself, I believed what I was told. I thought Mademoiselle Marie cared for you, and I—well, I gave up in despair. We have all been deceived, but I have acted like a fool."

The captain stood still in the middle of the road twisting his moustache, and the young pair kept silence, like culprits awaiting their sentence. Loigerot pulled at his moustache unmercifully, but it brought him no aid in the shape of counsel; he had hardly known till now how fond he had become of Marie, and it was very bitter to him to lose her. All at once he broke into a laugh—it was hardly cheerful, it sounded so derisive.

"You call yourself a fool, do you, monsieur? For a fool you seem to have done very well for yourself. It seems to me you have known how to arrange matters to your own advantage. *I* was the fool to be persuaded into thinking of a wife so much younger than myself . . . . Mademoiselle Marie," he said slowly, "I forgive you. I will not force myself upon you; but it is harder to me than—than you know—I—I am very fond of you, Mademoiselle Marie."

"Ah, monsieur, how good you are!" she caught his hand and pressed it between both hers.

But he drew it away. "There, there, child," he said. "Leave me alone, it seems to me you have been hardly used by your cousin—the old hag. I am not going to forgive the way she has used me. She has

behaved shamelessly, she shall pay for it all;
I am going back to tell her she is an old
devil. Come with me, mademoiselle."

He looked at Marie as if he were not
aware of Engemann's presence, but the
young man seized his hand.

"You are a trump, captain," he said;
"not one in a hundred would have been
so generous."

Loigerot drew his hand away roughly.
"I have nothing to do with you, monsieur.
You are nobody. Not worth that," he
snapped his fingers with contempt. "What
I shall do is for Mademoiselle Marie, and
for her alone."

"I feel that you have cause to despise
me," Rudolf said, "and I feel too that only
you, monsieur, have power to shield Marie
from Madame Bobineau's anger."

Loigerot shrugged his shoulders.

"I make no promises, but I think I have

power over the old woman. But with you, monsieur, I have nothing to do—absolutely nothing."

Then he turned his back on Engemann, and taking Marie's hand he tucked it under his arm.

"Mademoiselle," he said gravely, "I am at your service, if you will do me the honour to accept any help I can give you. Come along."

Marie had strained her courage to the utmost while she pleaded with the captain. Now she could hardly keep back her tears, and her fingers trembled so much that the good man was deeply touched.

"Courage, mademoiselle, all shall go well," he said. He pulled out his handkerchief and blew his nose violently.

Rudolf Engemann thought it was wiser to follow at a little distance. It was natural, he thought, that the sight of him should irritate the captain; his old esteem for Loigerot had come back, and he felt implicit trust in him.

"Mademoiselle Marie," said the captain as they walked on, "I am very angry with Madame Bobineau, and, I promise you, I shall not spare her; but she has cause to be angry with you, and be sure she will not spare you. Two wrongs will never make one right; but I may be able to quiet her; she is too wise or crafty to quarrel with me."

"Oh! I don't know how to thank you," said Marie in broken words; "you are very good to me, and I will pray that you may be rewarded for your kindness, and that you may soon find a girl more deserving than I am to marry."

He broke into a hearty laugh.

"Not if I know it, my beauty. In truth, I am too old for courting; this kind of thing is

too much trouble for me; it excites me more
than soldiering did. I did very well before
I saw you, and in future I shall let well
alone. Ah! here is the bridge! We shall
find Madame Bobineau at the further end
of it. Courage, my little girl; remember
Achille Loigerot is your friend."

CHAPTER IV.

"RUN TO EARTH."

> " He that is thy friend indeed,
> He will help thee at thy need."
> *Passionate Pilgrim.*

> " The gods are just, and of our pleasant vices
> Make instruments to scourge us."
> *King Lear.*

MADAME BOBINEAU had grown very tired of waiting.

"I am a fool to stop in this draughty place, just because that old captain bid me stay," she grumbled to herself; "it is not safe to sit here in the night air; it is enough to give me rheumatism. A plague

upon girls, and men too ! It is inconceivable
what a trouble they are.   Good Lord ! that
at my age I should be ordered about as if I
were a school-girl ! "

She tried to console herself with a big
pinch of snuff ; then she sat shivering and
grumbling.   Her thoughts soon went back
to Marie.   What could have become of the
naughty, headstrong girl ?   It was in-
credible that she could have behaved so
badly, though as to that, all girls were alike
untrustworthy ; still, she had been better
than most of them till now.

The old woman had restrained her anger
against the girl before the captain ; but she
felt furious as she thought of Marie's base
ingratitude.   She did not believe that she
was still in the gardens—but here Madame
Bobineau found herself pulled up short in
her meditations.   Where could Marie have
gone ?   She had no friends in Berne ; she

could not stay out all night, she was not bad enough for that.

All at once the old woman remembered that when she asked what had become of Monsieur Engemann, Madame Riesen had said he was going to walk home.

"Mon Dieu!" she cried out in sudden terror, "suppose they meet."

The old woman began to shake as if she had ague; her terror lifted the hair from her forehead, and she wrung her withered hands in despair at the idea that suggested itself. It was too wicked, too infamous, that two meritorious and honourable persons like Madame Carouge and Captain Loigerot should have their feelings outraged for the sake of a chit like Marie.

"Engemann is only a fool, but that does not lessen the danger," she said, in her anger. "Those big men are always fools; they are like lambs, they do all that a woman tells them to do. The forward chit has implored him to take pity on her, and— merciful Heaven! what may not have happened? I shall be ruined; I must be quick, or Madame Carouge will think I had a hand in it. She must be told directly."

She rose up quickly; she forgot her fatigue, her promise to the captain to await his return, and she went hobbling down the road till at last she came to the turning that led to the Hôtel Beauregard. The long street was as quiet as the grave; but when she reached the clock-tower she saw Moritz the waiter standing outside the entrance to the hotel, looking about as if he expected some one.

" Good evening, madame."

His eyebrows rose with surprise as the old woman turned to come in.

" Madame is in her parlour. I can see

her," she said, more as a statement than as a question.

Moritz bowed and turned to lead the way, while she followed slowly.

The impulse which had driven her to seek Madame Carouge was already checked by the fear that now overcame her. She knew how the widow could look and speak when she was angry, and Madame Bobineau's knees grew weak at the remembrance. She felt that she had been fool-hardy to bring such tidings, and she had half resolved to tell Moritz she would not intrude on his mistress, when she heard him announce her. It was evident that Madame Carouge was at the window of her room, and retreat had become impossible.

"Madame Bobineau!" she heard the widow say in a wondering tone, and the old glover turned the corner and met her at the open door.

The lamps were lighted, and the gold fish, swimming in the basin of the fountain, showed brilliantly through the overhanging ferns and palms. Madame Carouge had laid aside her bonnet; her beautiful head was slightly thrown back as she nodded to the old woman.

"Ah, how do you do again?" She spoke languidly; then, as soon as Moritz had departed, she closed the door and the window, and turned sharply to Madame Bobineau. "What are you sighing and panting about? Has anything happened, madame?" she said. She did not even ask her to sit down.

"I will rest if you please; I am tired to death." Madame Bobineau dropped into a chair. In spite of her alarm the old woman saw that the beauty was moved out of her ordinary self-possession, and this gave her confidence.

"I can go no further—pouf!—I seem to have been running about for hours trying to find that child."

"Do you mean Marie?"

Madame Carouge had remained standing, but now she put her hand on the back of a chair. She looked pale, Madame Bobineau thought.

"Yes, madame. That wicked old man deceived us. Marie did not go home with him; he says he knows nothing about her. While he turned his head, he says, she ran away — he missed her all at once in the gardens. Now I ask you, dear madame, is this likely? A timid girl like that would not go away alone among so many people. What does it all mean? I want your advice. What am I to do? How am I to find her?"

"Where is Captain Loigerot? Is he outside? I will see him, and question him." The widow spoke severely. "He is the

person to explain all this. Marie was left
with him. I saw her on his arm, smiling
and looking as happy as possible under his
admiring glances."

"You saw her?" Madame Bobineau
pricked up her ears; her way was becoming
easier.

"Yes, I was walking with Monsieur
Engemann. We both saw her, and we
both offered our congratulations to her and
to Captain Loigerot."

"Ah!" and then Madame Bobineau
checked herself. The mystery was becoming clearer. She half closed her sly
old eyes while she pictured to herself the
girl's vexation; no doubt Marie had run
away to avoid the sight of this happy pair.

Madame Carouge no longer held her head
erect. The old woman, seated at a little
distance on the sofa, was roused to attention
by her silence; she watched her with the
intensity of a cat sure of its prey, though

in Madame Bobineau's eyes a glitter of fear was mingled with the tense gaze she kept on the pale, anxious face of the widow.

"Where is Captain Loigerot?" suddenly said Madame Carouge. "Why don't you answer me?"

"He went back to the gardens to look for Marie. He said the child might be there still; he told me I was to wait at the bridge; but, mon Dieu! I could wait no longer in the dark. I was too anxious, and I wanted your advice, dear madame."

Madame Carouge walked up and down the small room. She dared not speak lest the terrible fear, that racked her till it seemed as if she could no longer endure the pain it gave, should shape itself in words. By degrees she grew quieter, and when she spoke again to Madame Bobineau, the sharp-eyed old woman was surprised at her calm tone.

"I am trying to think for you, madame, and it is not easy," she said. "First, I must tell you that you have been greatly to blame—shamefully careless. You must remember, I warned you that you were not fit to be the guardian of such a girl as Marie, and that the 'Red Glove' was not a fit place for her. Hush! you must not interrupt!" She fixed her eyes imperiously on Madame Bobineau, and the colour came back to her own face. "Marie will be found," she said bitterly. "I feel sure the captain will discover her and bring her home. No doubt she got tired of him and slipped away. Now listen to me. You must tell the girl that you will not force on the marriage with Captain Loigerot at present, but that you cannot keep her at the 'Red Glove' after her disgraceful conduct. She has thrown away her character this evening. Do you understand? She has lost her character, she has disgraced you. You know it is possible the captain will be very angry, and no one can wonder if he is."

" Yes, but he will forgive her, he is very fond of the child," said Madame Bobineau. " He will not——"

" Be quiet, will you ?" and another frown silenced the old woman. "I will have your shop minded to-morrow, and you must see that child off to Lucerne, she must not stay another day in Berne. Take her back to her friends at St. Esprit. I will pay all expenses, and I will write to the Superior, and explain the affair to her. You understand ? Marie must not remain in Berne after to-morrow. I have your authority, I imagine, madame," she went on with a sneer, " for saying that the girl is bold and indiscreet, and requires training till she can conduct herself more modestly."

"How good you are!—always good, always beautiful." In her relief, Madame Bobineau took a huge pinch of snuff, and brought tears into her eyes. "Yes, indeed," she whimpered; "what you say is indeed true, dear lady. Marie is very forward. I have seen her look at that noble young man, Monsieur Engemann, in a way that— that had he not been devoted to you, might have led him to notice her. She was so vain; I believe she thought he admired her."

Madame Carouge made a quick step forward with her hand raised, and then she stopped abruptly.

"Peace, you vile old woman! How dare you sit there telling what is your own shame? At the first glimpse of such behaviour in the girl, you should have shut the artful hussy up in a room, and kept her on bread and water till you had sent her back to her convent. Why did you not come to me at once for advice? How do you know what has happened to-night? I am not sure that the wretched girl is fit to be admitted among those saintly Sisters again—and you are to blame for it all."

Madame Bobineau was really terrified; she crouched till her chin almost touched her knees. She felt as if those fierce black eyes shot lightning, and the words pelted her like a storm of hail.

"Yes, yes, madame, I have been to blame," she said feebly, "I will take her away; I will do all you say. What did you say I was to tell Marie?"

"Why do you not listen? You are not to say a word about my advice in the matter. You are to tell the girl she has lost her character by this misconduct; that you cannot keep her at the 'Red Glove,' and that she must go back at once to her convent. She will be glad enough to go to escape the captain's anger. I tell you that a few weeks of dull convent life, now that she has had a peep of the world, will make her thankful to marry him by-and-by. That is all I have to say. You can go now."

She stamped her foot impatiently.

At the door Madame Bobineau turned back. In her terror her snuff-box had slipped from her hand on to the sofa, and she felt sorely in need of its comfort.

Madame Carouge turned her back on her while she went to look for it, and stood bending over her desk till the old woman had disappeared.

Meantime Marie had reached her lodging. There had been a little more talk between her and the captain on the way; but lately they had been silent, and indeed the girl was exhausted with the varied emotions she had gone through during the evening. She longed to be alone.

Engemann followed them, but he felt

that it was wiser to leave Loigerot in peace. He was surprised and puzzled at what had happened; but still he felt he could trust implicitly the little round man who rolled along with Marie on his arm.

When they reached the door of her lodging, the captain took the girl's hand in his.

"My child," he said, "you have done well to trust me. I will be your friend. It would—aw—it would have been better for us all if you had trusted me at the beginning. Yes, Mademoiselle Marie, it would have been much better."

Marie held his hand a moment; then, before he could stop her, she bent down and kissed it. "Monsieur"—she was crying now—"you are too good, too kind to me. I am very, very grateful. I shall always love you."

Loigerot patted her shoulder. "There,

there," he said, "not too much of that, or
I may change my mind yet, little one, and
take you at your word."

He cleared his throat, and in quite another
voice he said to Engemann:

"Monsieur, you can say 'good-night' to
mademoiselle."

He stood by while they shook hands
formally; then, when the door of her
lodging had closed on Marie, he looked
at Rudolf from head to foot.

"You are a pretty fellow," he said,
slowly, "a very pretty fellow, Rudolf
Engemann. Grand diable! you quiet ones
play the deuce with the women; but you
ought to look happier than you do to
have won the favour of two such women
as these—eh, mon Dieu! I tell you so.
Well, what the devil do you mean to do
with the widow? Let me tell you you
have treated her very badly."

Certainly Rudolf Engemann did not look like a happy lover; he had a limp, dejected aspect as he returned the captain's humorous stare.

"Monsieur," he said, "you are right; I have behaved badly; I feel like a fool. But first of all I must beg your pardon— yes, I was very rude to you, unjust too, while you have been most generous and forbearing. Well, to-night I had grown desperate: if I had not found Marie miserable among the trees up at the Schänzli, I believe I should have gone on to the hotel, as I had promised, and I should have proposed to Madame Carouge."

The captain snapped his fingers triumphantly.

"Then you have not proposed to her? Mon Dieu! that is good news, thundering good news, indeed;" he slapped his leg emphatically. "You are wiser than I thought.

I fancied she had hooked you long ago,
and that you had been playing fast and
loose between her and my little Marie."
Then, as he looked at Engemann's troubled
face, "Tonnerre! what is the matter now?
You have got the love of a sweet, virtuous
girl. You do not deserve your good fortune,
my lad, if you cannot enjoy it," he said.

"I told you I was miserable and desperate," the young fellow said moodily,
"and—and although I did not propose in
so many words, I have paid Madame
Carouge more attention this evening than I
ever did before. I even said I would call
on her, I know she is even now expecting
me. I have behaved very badly to her;
what am I to do?"

They had walked on side by side, and
now they stood beneath the Red Glove.
It seemed to point its fat scarlet thumb
derisively at Engemann, and one might

have fancied that his words were echoed up there from its dark perch:

"What am I to do—to do?"

Rudolf looked so disconsolate that the captain forgot everything but his amusement; he stuffed his hands into his pockets, and laughed till the tears came to his eyes. As soon as he could speak he said:

"That is excellent. What are you to do? You should have counted the cost sooner. What are you to do? That is a pretty question for a smart Don Juan like you to put to a man of my years. I will tell you what you cannot do, my fine fellow. Ma foi! you cannot keep them both."

The captain laughed again till the Red Glove, in the faint night-wind, seemed to sway backward and forward in sympathy with his mirth.

Engemann turned impatiently away; the captain's laughter tried his temper.

"Well, monsieur, I am at your mercy; I know I have been foolish, but there seems only one way left. I must go to Madame Carouge and tell her the truth like a man; it is the fairest way. Good night."

And he went off into the darkness under the arcade.

"Hold! stop! stop! Are you mad!" and there was the captain panting and holding on to the skirts of the young fellow's coat. "What a devil of a pace! Whew!—stop—my fine fellow," he gasped.

It took Loigerot a few minutes to recover his breath; then he put his arm into Engemann's, and led him back to the "Red Glove." He opened the private door and pointed to him to go in.

"Upon my word!" he said. "I am a bachelor, but I might as well be a father, for the trouble I have had to-night among the set of you. Go upstairs quietly, my

boy, and get to bed as fast as you can ; and
then, if you can, go to sleep. *You* go to
the widow and tell her the truth! You
might as safely walk up to the mouth of
cannon in action as trust yourself with her
to-night." He stopped to laugh again.

"But my promise? I said I would see
her again to-night."

The captain looked at the young fellow
out of his half-closed eyes.

"Your promise! Pie-crust—you understand? You are as fit to see her, my
young friend, as a bird is to interview a
hungry cat. No, no ; you leave the widow
to me. She is a fine creature and full of
goodness, no doubt—but she is a widow
in love, and that is the devil. Poor thing!
I am sorry for her, though ; she has been
hardly used. But she and I are in the
same boat, and we must console each other.
Listen," he said, in his pompous manner,

"aw — I will manage the affair. I will let her sleep over it, and to-morrow I will bring her round famously ; it will be difficult, and—but don't you be afraid. There ! there ! be off. Be quiet, I tell you !"— as the young fellow began to pour out his gratitude. "I don't say I have forgiven you yet for robbing me of that sweet child ; you make her a good husband, that's all, and perhaps after a bit I'll forgive you. Now for the old hag; she shall get it," he said to himself, when the young fellow had gone upstairs, "for she has made all the mischief. I must find out if she has come in yet."

He lit a cigar, and then he called gently for Madame Bobineau. It was possible that she had gone home to bed as soon as he left her. But the gas in the entrance-passage was not lighted, and this was an unusual omission.

"No ; she has not come in," he said,

when he had stood for some time listening. He shut the door, and went out into the arcade to wait for the old woman.

He had not long to wait. Before she saw him, as he stood in the shadow of the arcade, he saw her crouching figure hobbling along. She was still trembling from the effect of her interview with Madame Carouge, and grumbling to herself, when all at once she looked up and perceived the captain standing at the door of her house.

"What have you done with Marie?" she said, angrily.

"Mademoiselle Peyrolles is safe in her lodging. Now listen to me. In future, Madame Bobineau, when you dispose of anything, be careful first to make sure that it does not belong to some one else. You have grossly deceived me in regard to that poor girl."

Madame Bobineau was tired and hungry,

and angry besides. All the temper sup-
pressed by the stronger passion of Madame
Carouge flew out rebelliously. She longed
to fly at the captain; she would have
pulled his hair and scratched his face if
the remembrance that he was her first-floor
lodger had not restrained her.

"Monsieur," she said, sullenly, "it is I
who have reason to complain. I trusted
you with Marie, and you lost her in the
gardens. However, I suppose you and she
have made it up; so I will say no more
about it to-night, but to-morrow I must
have an explanation."

"Sapristi! you bad old woman, is that
the way you take it? You will say no
more! You will have an explanation!" He
pulled himself together. "This is excellent, on my soul; how dare you talk in
this way to me? Nom de Dieu! Madame
Bobineau," he went on, with dignity,

"Mademoiselle Marie is my friend; I shall always have a great regard for her; but she will never be anything more than a friend to me. Poor little girl! you have used her shamefully; you had made her miserable; she ran away from me, but she shall not be scolded for it. I found her in the dark with her lover, Monsieur Engemann; so, you see, madame, if you wish to save her character, you must let the young people marry."

"Let them marry!" she shrieked. "Never! let her marry that clerk, never! never! Marie is under age, and I refuse my consent. I shall take her back to her convent to-morrow."

"Keep yourself quiet, you old fool," he said in a low voice, "do you want Madame Webern to know all that has happened? Come indoors, and light the lamp."

She obeyed sullenly.

"Good night, monsieur," she said when

the lamp was lighted. "You will have changed your mind by to-morrow."

"Stop a bit," he said, and he placed himself in front of the door of her room, his bulk filling up the narrow passage so that if she had tried she could with difficulty have squeezed by him. " You had better understand me distinctly. I never change a purpose, madame, unless I find that events prevent me from carrying it out. I meant to marry your cousin, but you yourself have made this impossible."

" I !—oh, monsieur, you have been grossly imposed on. Oh, that wicked little hussy shall pay for this ! "

" Now listen to me, and do not you venture to speak against the child. I am tired, and I want to go to bed. So these are the last words I have to say. You only are to blame." He had taken his cigar out of his mouth, and he used it to emphasise his words as he spoke. " If

I find that you have said so much as one unkind word to Mademoiselle Marie, I will leave your lodgings, and I will let Lenoir and Riesen and every one in Berne know of your infamous conduct. How dare you tell me that Marie was fond of me and willing to marry me, when at the same time you told her that she was fond of young Engemann?—and then you leave her in the gardens alone with me." He shook his cigar menacingly. "You have not many friends; you will not have one if I open my mouth, and I will do it unless you obey me. Marie has compromised herself with that young man — very well. They shall be formally betrothed, and then she can go back to her convent till he is able to marry her, for marry her he must. Now, madame, you know the position. Do you understand ?"

She understood very well, and she

struggled to resist, but her courage failed her.

"You are very hard on me," she whimpered.

"On the contrary, I let you off easily. And, mark you, madame, if, when Engemann is ready to marry your cousin, you refuse your consent, or try any more trickery"— he frowned till his moustache quivered, and he looked surprisingly fierce — "bon; I shall then know how to deal with you, and I shall expose the abominable conduct you have used toward me and Mademoiselle Marie to all the world."

He turned his back on her, and walked deliberately upstairs.

Madame Bobineau sat down on the lowest step, and wrung her hands in impotent fury.

"Horrid, wicked, old man! I hate him!" she muttered; "I will—no—no—

he pays me twice as much as any lodger ever paid before, and he is a friend of Madame Carouge. Oh, if he were only some one else."

Madame Bobineau was unable to enjoy her supper, and she went to bed in a miserable state of mind.

CHAPTER V.

HOW LOIGEROT MANAGED THE WIDOW.

"Men were deceivers ever."—*Song.*

"And will he not come again?
And will he not come again? . . .
He never will come again."
                    Song—SHAKESPEARE.

MORITZ the waiter looked disturbed as he went about his duties this morning. The hectic flush had spread over his hollow cheeks, and there was an angry brightness in his melancholy brown eyes. Evidently something had gone wrong with the head-waiter of the Beauregard. If you followed the direction of his eyes you would soon have discovered that every time he went

Q 2

in and out of the breakfast-room he glanced
across at his mistress's parlour. Moreover,
he made several needless journeys up and
down stairs, so that he might get a good
look at her.

Indeed Moritz was greatly troubled,
he could not imagine what had happened
to Madame Carouge. Last night he thought
she had looked superb when she started for
the Schänzli, and she had come in blooming
and radiant; what could have happened to
change her this morning into a pale, heavy-
eyed statue, so silent and preoccupied that
she seemed unable to attend to business,
and had sent away her breakfast untouched ?

Moritz felt that some one had to bear the
blame of this change, and he hesitated
between Madame Bobineau and Rudolf
Engemann.

When Madame Carouge came in last
night, she had told Moritz she would
receive Monsieur Engemann when he

called, and the waiter had felt full of
jealous trouble. He adored his beautiful
mistress, and he felt that virtually he was
master at the Beauregard ; the idea that
this bank clerk, some years younger than
himself, was to be set over his head, was
exasperating. When Engemann failed to
appear, and Madame Bobineau paid that
short, stormy visit which had attracted his
keen attention, Moritz did not know what
to think.

He had heard all the chatter that Lenoir
could furnish him with ; and indeed the
gossips of Berne had been living on the
events of these double courtships during
the past week. Moritz suspected that Engemann was playing a double game —
flirting with Marie, while he intended to
marry the widow—and this idea had increased his dislike of the fair young
giant. Rudolf's coolness and self-possession
always irritated the nervous man, whose

movements were as rapid as his wits were sharp. That "such a carcase," as he termed Engemann, without any *savoir faire* should aspire to beautiful, wealthy Madame Carouge, was most audacious. He did not want her to marry, and that she should encourage such a dull half-hearted lover as he appeared to the waiter was astounding ; at this idea Moritz always shrugged his shoulders. He knew that his mistress had had a bad time with Carouge ; poor soul ! she was not to be blamed if she thought that his opposite in all respects was likely to make her happy. " Women only look outside," Moritz told himself.

But what, he asked himself, could have happened to change her in these few hours ? —unless Madame Bobineau had brought her an unpleasant message from Engemann.

The widow had closed both door and window during the old woman's visit, but

Moritz had heard fragments of the wordy battle through the key-hole of the door of communication between his own little office and his mistress's parlour. This morning, when breakfast was over and Engemann did not appear, the head waiter became certain that something had gone wrong; he could do nothing but rush to the entrance at intervals, and stare expectantly down the street.

The morning went on, and all the early breakfasters departed. There was a lull in the house, but Madame Carouge did not take advantage of this, as she often did, to go upstairs to her room.

She sat at her desk trying to add up the same long column of figures which had occupied her all the morning. She had stayed up till midnight waiting for Engemann, and then she had gone to bed heart-sick and weary, but she had not slept. She had guessed at some of the truth while Madame Bobineau told her story; but for all that she had not given up the hope of marrying Rudolf Engemann. He was not to blame, poor fellow! How could he help it if that girl had thrown herself on his protection, and asked him to deliver her from the captain? He might even have felt obliged to see her home. "The old woman has pressed Marie too hard," she said; "she is a commonplace tyrant without any tact, and the girl, in despair, has flung herself on Rudolf Engemann's protection."

The keen torment roused by this idea robbed her of sleep, but she assured herself that Rudolf had gone too far with her to draw back. "He is not a man to kiss a woman's hand, and to look at her as he looked at me, if he were only trifling. No, he could not trifle with me; he is too true

and simple." She repeated this over and
over again, but she could not succeed in
quieting her anxiety.

Matters looked worse to her this morning.
She had risen early, and dressed herself with
extra care ; she sent word, however, to Lenoir
that she did not want his services : she was
really afraid of his keen eyes. Her hope was
that Rudolf would appear earlier than usual ;
but he had not even come to breakfast, and
she knew he was already due at the bank.
Last night she had got rid of her anger on
Madame Bobineau ; now, as she waited, her
colour began to return, and her eyes, in
spite of their heavy lids, looked dangerous.

"I will not judge him," she kept on
saying vehemently to herself. " His conduct is of course very strange ; he ought to
have kept his promise, but the dear fellow
may have reasons ; I will not say anything
I may be sorry for later on."

But her heart beat more quickly, and
her colour flickered at the mere sound of
a footstep; at last she gave up the figures
she was trying to add up as hopeless,
and seated herself on the sofa with a news-
paper, but after a few minutes it lay in her
lap.

Presently Moritz put his head in at the
window. "Madame, will you see Monsieur
Loigerot?"

She looked up joyfully.

"By all means; show him in." The
thought came that Rudolf was too modest
to plead for himself—the captain was his
ambassador. "Good morning, captain"—
Madame Carouge went forward and shook
hands cordially, when she saw Loigerot's
bald head bowing down in the doorway.
"You are early this morning, monsieur."

Then, as he still lingered in the doorway,
she pointed to a chair near the sofa.

But the captain did not sit down; he stood before her with his hat in his hand.

" Pardon me, madame—aw—I have a few important words to say to you privately ; that is—aw—if you will condescend to listen."

He looked so absurd, so nervous, as he half closed his eyes and tugged at his moustache, that the widow could not help smiling.

" With the greatest pleasure, monsieur," she said, in her most charming way. " Will you have the goodness to shut the door ? "

" She is divine to look at," Loigerot said to himself ; " but I believe she's got a devil of a temper.   Engemann is well out of it— and I wish I was well out of it too."

The captain felt that he understood the widow, but he also felt that he did not understand how to manage her.

" Well, madame, I am not sure about the

pleasure you may derive from my—aw—
communication," he said nervously; "but
you are full of charity and sweetness—I
am sure you are, and—and I want to ask
you to do an act of charity. I—I——"

He felt stuck here, he looked at her
helplessly.

"A charity, monsieur? Is it a case of
distress? Yes, indeed, monsieur, you may
count on me; I am always ready to help
distress. It is so sad to let others go on
suffering," she said pathetically, "when we
have the means of helping them." She
was at once relieved and disappointed; he
had not come, then, on the errand she hoped.

"What is it you wish?" she said. "Tell
me, monsieur, you can command my purse."

Loigerot had gone on tugging at and
twisting his moustache, and now he felt
that the widow was looking keenly at him,
searching him through and through.

Drops started out on the captain's forehead, and his tongue felt stiff and useless.
All at once the thought of Marie's imploring, tear-stained face came to help him.

"You are very kind and quite right,
madame, and I have a case of real distress
to lay before you which you have power
to help—not with money, however. I want
you to befriend little Marie Peyrolles—to
take her part against Madame Bobineau."

Madame Carouge's face grew set in a
moment, and her eyes looked hard. She
shook her head.

"Madame Bobineau is the child's
guardian," she said repressively. "I cannot interfere."

She began to feel that the ground was
slipping from under her feet.

"You are right again, madame," he said
pompously, "perfectly right. Madame
Bobineau is her guardian; but she is—

well, I let her off easy when I say she is a
bad, treacherous woman. She has behaved
shamefully to the poor little girl."

Madame Carouge laughed; but there
was no music in her laugh. "No, no,
monsieur; you are too hard on the poor
old woman. It is easy to see that you
have been misinformed. Girls are—well
I cannot, of course, speak unfavourably
to you of Mademoiselle Marie. I will only
say I fear she is prejudiced against her
kind, old cousin; but why need you
come to me, monsieur? You are surely
Marie's best adviser."

"I"—he had felt this question coming;
he put up both hands; then he shrugged
his shoulders. "Now for it," he thought,
and like the swimmer who shuts his eyes as
he plunges into the water, he went on, without looking at Madame Carouge. "Pardon
me, I forgot, madame, you do not know;

there is still something to be explained to
you. That old woman has deceived the
poor child as much as she has deceived me.
Luckily I made a discovery last night."
The widow had put her hand before her
mouth to hide a yawn; but at his last
words she listened attentively. "Yes,
madame, a discovery which will, perhaps,
surprise you as much as it surprised me."
He raised his hand and pointed a stumpy
forefinger at the widow. "It is not me that
Mademoiselle Marie wishes to marry, it is
Monsieur Rudolf Engemann; and I have
given her up to him."

Madame Carouge rose up, her eyes
flashed out brightly on the captain, then
she laughed, but the laugh was not natural.

"Nonsense! You have been listening
to gossip, monsieur; you have got your
story upside down; I cannot let you talk
in this way. I think you are very un-

grateful to talk of giving up the little girl after all the trouble I have taken for you. As to Monsieur Engemann," she said derisively, "I happen to know, on good authority, that he—loves some one else. You have made a very foolish mistake, Captain Loigerot, and the sooner you set it right the better for all parties."

The captain reddened at the scorn in her voice.

"I have made no mistake," he said roughly. "I saw and heard too last night and judged for myself."

"You saw!" she said vehemently. "What are you talking about?"

He raised his hand. "Calm yourself, madame; you and I are older than these young people are; let us be more reasonable. I have given up my hopes. Will the 'some one else' you speak of be less generous?" She turned angrily away and walked across the room. Her loss of self-control had given the captain courage, she would feel ashamed of herself, he thought, and be easier to manage; he rubbed his hands, he considered his last sentence had been a very telling manœuvre. He followed the widow as she walked. "I believe," he said, "that Monsieur Engemann has not offered himself to the 'some one else.' Ah, madame, think how young they are—they are so well matched—and think how they love one another." He put his hand on her arm. "I will tell you, madame, what is to be done."

"Well, monsieur?"

She turned round, she was listening eagerly with half-closed eyes and dilated nostrils.

Loigerot felt encouraged by her silence. "Yes, yes! madame, they love each other dearly; you should have seen them together

when 1 found them last night—poor love-
birds. I was very stern at first, mind you, I
was very angry, and I told them so ; but they
behaved well, and they threw themselves on
my compassion, and—aw—I saw I must give
in to the force of circumstances." Then he
raised himself on tiptoe, and whispered,
in what he meant for a coaxing tone:
" Surely, ' some one else' does not want
to keep a man who loves another woman."

The captain was not very steady on tiptoe, and as he looked up earnestly at the
widow, a stinging box on the ear nearly
sent him off his legs.

" Take that for your pains, you chattering
busybody," said Madame Carouge, looking
splendid in her fury, as she towered above
the astounded man.

" Tonnerre !" he put one hand to his ear,
and the other to where his sword used
to hang. Then he drew himself up and

smiled. "Madame, I thank you for the lesson. I am consoled for the loss of my little wife. Marie is only a kitten at present, but you—aw—you have shown me what she might have grown to. Madame, I—I have the honour to take my leave."

CHAPTER VI.

"PAPA LOISEROT."

"Nature had formed him of the best and kindliest clay, had tempered it with her own milk, and breathed into it the sweetest spirit; she had made him all gentle, generous, and humane; she had filled his heart with trust and confidence."—STERNE.

IT is a holiday in Berne, and although most of the shops are open, there are plenty of townspeople in the streets dressed in their best and bent on enjoying themselves. Posters here and there announce that in the evening there will be a concert and a display of fireworks at the Schänzli; but the gay groups are now on their way to the bear-pit or the Enge. And already numbers of strangers have come in by railway, and are sauntering up the town.

A short, stout man is walking up and down beside the station with a sort of rolling gait. Captain Loigerot is as fond of the sunshine as ever; but he looks unusually radiant even for such a bright June day. He has scarcely aged in the seven years since his memorable parting with Madame Carouge; though his hair is a trifle grayer. Friends pass him, and he greets them in a hearty, cheery voice. Now he crosses the street and consults the clock in the library, and then with a broad smile he makes straight for the entrance of the station; he stands there with his head thrown back, his legs planted wide apart, and his moustaches quivering with expectation.

A rush of passengers comes out and disperses itself into the various conveyances and through the streets. Then people come out more scantily, in twos and threes; he peers curiously at them as they pass. But now he makes a forward movement, and nearly stumbles over a respectable-looking bonne in a round straw hat who leads a little girl by each hand.

"It is monsieur le capitaine," says the bonne; and she stops and makes a curtsey, then she draws her charges back into a corner so that they may greet monsieur le capitaine.

He is stooping down over them, his face growing purple with excitement.

"Good day, my beauties," he says. "How well they look! Were there ever such little angels! And they have come all the way from Fribourg to see papa Loigerot; how hungry they must be!"

The two small creatures look at him frankly as they hold up their faces to be

kissed. " Bojour, papa Loiserot," they say ;
he is plainly an old acquaintance.

They are certainly a lovely pair, fair-
skinned, with fair hair hanging down their
backs in long plaits. They are prettily
dressed too in white, with blue ribbons in
their white straw hats. Marie, the eldest,
has eyes to match her ribbons ; but Célie,
a tiny creature of three, is the image of her
mother ; and Loigerot gives her an extra
kiss as he bends over her.

" Is Célie very hungry, eh ? " he half
closes his eyes, and the child laughs
joyously.

" Yes, papa Loiserot," she says in a little
soft voice. " Célie is very hungry."

" That is what I thought, you see." He
winks at the smiling old bonne; he takes first
Célie's hand, and then Marie's, and prepares
to start. " It is absolutely necessary, Elise,
we should go on very fast to the cake shop,

or it is possible that Mademoiselle Célie may eat me up by the way."

This seems such a huge joke of "papa Loiserot's," that the two pretty creatures laugh across him at one another, till their walk becomes as rolling as the captain's.

"Help yourselves, my jewels," he says, when they reach the cake shop; and, while they swallow cream and chocolate tarts, more delicious than any they ever dreamed of, he buys each of them a big box of bonbons.

During all this time, and until they have finished their cakes, the captain's face has been radiant; he cannot take his eyes from the children, their pretty little ways, their merry jests and laughter keep him in an excitement of delight which breaks out in various expressions; but, as they turn into the streets again, the bonne suggests that Madame Eugemann wished

her little girls to go to the "Red Glove,"
to see Madame Bobineau.

Captain Loigerot does not smile at this.

"Why should they visit the old——"

He is on the point of calling Madame
Bobineau "old devil," but the sweet little
faces gazing up into his with sudden amaze-
ment check him just in time.

"Madame Bobineau can wait," he says
roughly. "There is no time now. I mean
to take them back to the station this afternoon and then you can start a little sooner,
if this—this visit must be paid. You need
only be five minutes about it; the dear
little angels did not come to Berne to spend
their time in that dismal old glove shop."

The bonne curtseys, she is devoted to the
captain, and it is evident to her that he
objects to the mistress of the "Red Glove."

"Come along, my darlings," he looks
down into the little faces beside him, and

his serenity returns. "We are going to
dine now, but you shall get an appetite
first. We will see the great clock on the
tower, and the ogre at the fountain, and,
after dinner, the bears. Yes, yes, little
Célie, you do well to hold my hand tight,
for the greedy ogre eats up little ones all day
long, and you would make a dainty mouth-
ful for him. There — there, do not be
frightened, my angel, I will take care of you."

He rolls along the street again with a
child on each side of him, and when he
has shown them the clock and the fountain
he turns into the Beauregard, where Moritz
stands waiting. The waiter's sunken cheeks
grow brighter at the pretty sight.

"Ah, monsieur," he says, as he looks at
Célie, "she is as like Ma'mzelle Marie as
one drop of water is like another; and this
other is like Monsieur Engemann. Ma foi!
she should have been a boy, she would have

made as tall and fine a fellow as monsieur
her father"—it is surprising how much
higher Rudolf stands in the opinion of
both Moritz and Monsieur Riesen since his
marriage with Marie Peyrolles.

"Go along with you," the captain says.
"I like girls best; these are my grandchildren, Moritz, and they are as hungry
as the ogre—eh, my little one? What is
the matter, my jewel?"

For, at the word ogre, Célie's eyelashes
have begun to twinkle and she pinches
her nurse's apron between her tiny fingers;
that terrible spectacle of the voracious ogre
on the fountain has given her a shock.

"Poor little pet, is she frightened?" the
captain pats her cheek with his fat fingers,
"but she wants her dinner," and he leads
the way into the breakfast-room, where he
has ordered a dainty meal for his guests.

"Ah," he says to himself as he turns

his back on the bureau, the fountain, and its green surroundings. "Once upon a time I should have taken them in there to see Chéri—Tonnerre!" he bustles on into the restaurant, "what am I thinking of? Even if madame had not left Berne she would have turned her back on these little ones. Ah! she was a fine creature, though perhaps a trifle violent, but she was hardly dealt by—I excused her."

Loigerot is disappointed that his guests have so little appetite for the excellent fare he has provided ; and for a few moments he becomes low-spirited when the bonne resolutely says that they may not drink champagne. Both Marie and her sister are thinking so much about the bears that they are impatient of the time spent by the bonne, who greatly enjoys her good meal.

"I am ready, papa Loigerot," Marie says ; but Célie slips her little hand into the captain's and looks up at him with a timid smile.

"Yes, you are right," he says to Moritz, whom he has summoned to ask if the carriage is ready. " She will be as charming as her mother, and she will make some one's heart ache before she is twenty." He sighs and looks serious for a moment.

The children give a cry of delight when they cross the river. Then the carriage stops and Loigerot lifts out first Marie and then Célie, and then politely hands out the bonne.

Hand in hand the captain and the two little girls reach the platform, and Marie and Célie cry out for joy at the sight of the toy bears.

"Papa Loigerot, see here," and "papa Loiserot, look at this one," and then they clap their little hands, and their ripples of happy laughter send the captain into ecstasy.

He buys bears of all sizes, white, brown, and black; he gives the bonne a huge parcel to carry, he also carries one himself under one arm, for his hands still hold those of the little girls. And now Marie is pulling him in the direction of the bear-pit, which the bonne has pointed out to her.

Since he has seen her fear of the painted stone ogre, the captain is a little nervous about Célie and the bears.

He clasps her little hand tightly as they reach the edge of the pit.

There are the monsters, begging, fawning, laughing in the same hideous fashion that they did years ago.

There is a little wail, "Ah!" and Célie clasps her arms tightly round the captain's leg and bursts into terrified sobs.

"Hush, hush, my darling, my poor little angel!" says Loigerot. " Marie, are you afraid to stand there alone if you loose my hand a moment?"

"No, papa Loigerot," the child says, "I am not afraid at all; poor little Célie is a coward, you know."

"She is a darling!" and now that he has both hands free, the troubled captain raises Célie in his arms and soothes her as if she were a baby. "Do not scold her, Elise," he says, as the nurse scolds the little one for her panic; "it is natural. How do you know that you too would not cry, if you were a little one, the first time you saw the ugly brutes? Go and buy some carrots for Ma'mzelle Marie to throw to them."

Marie was delighted; she was a little afraid, but she tried to show her courage by flinging carrot after carrot into the huge grinning mouth of the biggest bear. The applause she roused from the bystanders roused Célie from her fears; she forgot her terrors of the bear as she witnessed Marie's success.

"Aha! Good day again, Lenoir," the captain says. "Look here; these are my grandchildren; they belong to Monsieur Rudolf Engemann, of Fribourg."

"One might know that, certainly," says Lenoir; "this little lady is the very portrait of her father."

Marie looks up approvingly at the bird-like barber; she is elated by her triumph over her fear. "Mamma says I ought to be a boy," she says, "and papa says when he dies I shall have to take care of mamma and Célie."

Célie sits upright in the captain's arms.

"You are too little to take care of mamma," she says. Then she nestles her face into the captain's shoulder. "Papa

Loiserot will take care of me and of mamma too."

The captain hugs the child closely, and kisses her on both cheeks.

"Do you hear, monsieur?" Lenoir laughs. "That is perhaps a prophecy. Do you remember what Madame Carouge said after that famous evening at the Schänzli?"

The captain looks pensive. "You told me, my good friend, but I have forgotten. What was it?"

"She said that a certain young person, who shall be nameless, if you please, monsieur, was a little fool, and that she would have been wiser if she had chosen the man who loved her instead of the man she loved herself."

Lenoir looks significantly at the small Marie, whose blue eyes stare hard at him.

"Ah, poor woman, she had a temper," the captain says, and he sighs; "but she was a fine creature, we can ill spare her from Berne."

"Bah," says Lenoir, " she is wise, she has gone on her travels ; she knows well enough that Moritz is devoted to her interests, and that the Beauregard will not suffer during these years of absence. She is enjoying her liberty. She will return cured and happy, and she will perhaps find," says Lenoir, slapping his expanded chest, "that she left a possible happiness behind her."

The captain's eyes twinkle.

"It is possible, my friend, that she may bring home a husband with her," he says.

Lenoir makes a grimace. "I will say good morning, monsieur le capitaine," and he bows and passes on.

Lenoir has revived painful memories in the captain, but he soon shakes them aside, he does not want to lose a minute of the society of his dear little girls. He smiles at them lovingly. "Come, my darlings, let us say good day to the bears."

"I am glad that cross man is gone," Célie says, "he is as ugly as the bears; he is like an ugly dickey-bird, papa Loiserot."

THE END.

CHARLES DICKENS AND EVANS, CRYSTAL PALACE PRESS.